The Adventures of
Captain Al Scabbard
#1

The Adventures of Captain Al Scabbard #1

by
Lawrence J. Crabb, Jr.
and
Lawrence J. Crabb, Sr.

MOODY PRESS

CHICAGO

© 1981 by
THE MOODY BIBLE INSTITUTE
OF CHICAGO

Library of Congress Cataloging in Publication Data

Crabb, Lawrence J.
  The Adventure of Captain Al Scabbard #1.

  SUMMARY: Four adventures of crime fighter Al Scabbard whose close relationship with God helps him achieve his accomplishments.

  1. Mystery and detective stories. 2. Christian life—Fiction. I. Crabb, Lawrence James, 1912- joint author. II. Title.
PZ7.C84Ac   [Fic]   80-27223
ISBN 0-8024-0280-1

3 4 5 6 7 Printing/LC/Year 87 86 85 84 83 82

Printed in the United States of America

Contents

PREFACE

You are about to read a series of stories that we made up. Just like television shows about the Dukes of Hazard or movies about Luke Skywalker, these stories never really happened.

It's important to know when something is true and when something is not true. When you read in the Bible that David killed a nine-foot-tall giant or that a carpenter named Jesus raised a man from the dead, you are reading about events that actually took place years ago.

If you had lived in ancient Israel and had been watching from a nearby hilltop, you could have seen a young boy really walk up to Goliath, hurl a stone from his sling, and kill the giant. You could have then walked up to Goliath's dead body and touched it, just like you can touch your own knee right now. And if you had been alive years ago and had been a friend of two women named Mary and Martha, perhaps you would have gone to the funeral when their brother Lazarus died. Four days later, if you were standing near the cave where Lazarus was buried, you would have heard Jesus call out, "Lazarus, come forth." With your own eyes you would have actually seen a man who had died come out of his grave and talk with his sisters just like your friends talk to you. Those stories are true. They really happened exactly as the Bible says they happened.

The adventures of Captain Al Scabbard are different. We invented them in our minds, then wrote them down in this book for you to enjoy. But even though there never was a real Al Scabbard, these stories about him and his friends might be important for you to read. Let us tell you why.

Have you ever seen the Dukes of Hazard talk to God about their problems? Did the Incredible Hulk ever pray that God would cure him so he could live a normal life? Do you remember *Star Wars* hero Luke Skywalker carrying his Bible with him into his spaceship? Of course not.

You might start thinking that the really neat heroes that are so much fun to read about or watch on TV or in the movies don't really need God in their lives. They seem to get along quite well without ever trusting in the Lord or reading the Bible. And it may be that most of them don't think that God is very important. But they're wrong.

We want to introduce you to a man who is

tough, smart, and finds himself living through one exciting adventure after another. But this man is different from other heroes. He believes that there really is a God; he talks to God about whatever he does; and he wants more than anything else to live for God.

We thought it was about time that you could read about a special kind of person who really understands what life is all about. Now remember, as you read these adventures, Captain Al Scabbard never really existed. But the God he believed in is real. We didn't make Him up.

INTRODUCTION

This is the story of Captain Al Scabbard.
Perhaps you have never heard of Scabbard. That is
not surprising. Captain Scabbard always did the
best he could to avoid the spotlight. Not that did
not like recognition—he did. It was for that very
reason that he shied away from it so strongly.
Scabbard believed that once a man began living
for fame, he lived for little else.

No one who met Scabbard ever forgot him. His
dark brown, almost black, hair fell neatly over
most of his forehead. Thick sideburns, extending
about half an inch beneath the bottom of his ears,
silhouetted a face that looked more square than
oval because of a rather flat chin. At first glance,
you got the distinct impression that Scabbard was
a no-nonsense, let's-get-to-it sort of a man—and
he was.

Most people, except those who broke the law,
felt at ease around him. His dark eyes, nestled
beneath bushy brown eyebrows, sparkled with a
strangely intense warmth that made you feel com-

fortable and awed at the same time. Captain Scabbard was not impressively big, measuring about five feet ten inches tall with a solid yet not thickly-muscled physique. But one handshake made you quickly aware that behind that firm grasp was a reservoir of strength, available when needed. Although there was nothing really remarkable in his general appearance, there *was* something about him that you noticed. Or maybe "sensed" is a better word.

Have you ever met someone who tried to let you know how smart he was or how well he could perform on a basketball court or at a piano? Do you remember what your reaction was? You probably said to yourself, "What a show-off," and even if he really was smart or talented, you likely looked for all the things he could *not* do very well.

But the response of people to Al Scabbard was precisely the opposite. Rather than picking away at his faults (and Scabbard did have faults, including a few major ones), people tended to overlook them and to speak about his good points. The interesting thing is that Scabbard did not really try to impress anyone. But some people, usually the kind who live their lives through others, were so taken with Scabbard that they made up all sorts of wonderful stories about him.

One story I heard had Captain Scabbard outrunning a cheetah in the African jungle, on his way to bring medicine to a dying witch doctor who had earlier tried to kill him. But everyone knows that only Tony Cannon, Al's good friend, would have a chance of outrunning a cheetah.

Another of those fanciful stories told of the time that Al Scabbard knocked out two heavyweight prizefighters in less than three minutes. But that of course was another of Al's friends—Archie Cramer, the toughest, hardest-hitting boxer in the world, and it was *three* fighters he decked in under *two* minutes. (I hope I don't forget to tell you about the time Archie and Al entered the ring to fight one another. I was there to see it. Incredible!)

Scabbard told me of one story he had heard in which he was reported to have shot a dagger flying through the air from a distance of slightly less than three hundred feet. A would-be assassin employed by the Baron (you'll hear of him later) had hurled the deadly weapon at a foreign princess visiting our country. Now Scabbard is no amateur with a pistol, but it is commonly admitted that only Bob Culpepper, detective with the San Marlindo police department, could shoot that well.

Captain Scabbard was embarrassed and even a little annoyed by the wild tales that people were spreading about him, so when I approached him with the idea of recording his adventures in a book, he initially felt rather negative about it. But we discussed the idea of a book for several hours, reflecting on how God had chosen to work in so many unusual ways through his life and the lives of his friends. After praying about the matter for several days, Scabbard finally decided that writing these adventures for the general public to read might help some people realize just how big God really is.

Scabbard loaned me the three thick scrapbooks his wife, Sally, had carefully kept over the years, filled with newspaper clippings, magazine articles, letters of appreciation from people whom Scabbard had helped, awards from various groups (including several from our government), FBI reports detailing how Scabbard solved some of their most baffling cases, and a host of other records of Scabbard's most extraordinary life.

For six months I pored over the scrapbooks, organizing, editing, and rewriting the adventures contained in those pages. I spent another six months contacting every individual I could locate who had a "Scabbard story" to tell. And Captain Scabbard generously granted me hours of his time, filling in the bare spots with details that only Scabbard himself could possibly know.

As I began writing these adventures, it occurred to me that some readers just would not believe they ever happened. I had a little trouble myself with a few of the incidents. Although I'm a little embarrassed to admit it, I should tell you that whenever I could I carefully double-checked the stories I heard as well as the scrapbook records with other reliable sources.

Oh, yes, one more thing. Captain Scabbard insisted I include this at the beginning. These are his words:

"As you read these stories, remember that whatever good I have accomplished has been done by the strength and wisdom of the Lord. Without Him, I am nothing. If you are impressed with these adventures, be impressed with Him."

1

The Cabin in the Woods

Records from several New York newspapers indicate that the story you are about to read took place in the spring of 1957. Captain Scabbard was not certain whether it happened in '57 or '58, but the details of the adventure were vividly clear in his memory. As we relaxed together in two overstuffed rocking chairs placed just far enough away from the blaze in the fireplace, he closed his eyes and began telling me the story. When he mentioned the phone call he received that Thursday evening, which set this adventure in motion, I thought I noticed his jaw tightening a bit. The chilling adventure of the cabin in the woods was enough to unnerve even Captain Al Scabbard.

The story really began three weeks before that eventful phone call, in the home of a Mr. Leroy Hatchmire, successful businessman, husband, and father of three. The entire Hatchmire family was gathered in the living room of their suburban, two-story home, excitedly making plans for their upcoming camping trip to Yellow River Forest—everyone, that is, except blond-haired, nine-year-old Peter, the youngest of the three children. Peter was stretched out lazily on the couch, doing his best to look bored. The other family members were so busy studying maps and planning what to take that they did not notice Peter's yawns and sighs. After being ignored for too long, Peter spoke up.

"They don't even have a swimming pool where we're going. There'll be nothing to do but look at a bunch of dumb trees. What a blast."

Peter, his aunt once observed, seemed to enjoy complaining as much as other kids enjoy peanut butter and jelly sandwiches.

Glenda Hatchmire, Peter's mother, responded to his grumbling (as she usually did) with a lecture, this one on the virtues of cooperation.

"Peter," Mrs. Hatchmire started in her most patient tone. "A family works well together and has a good time only if each member tries his hardest to get along with each other. Remember, a family is a team, and we all must. . ."

As his mother droned on, Peter looked away and muttered something about "Mother's stupid sermons."

Details of the trip were eventually worked out to everyone's delighted satisfaction, everyone's except of course Peter's. Two weeks later, right on schedule, the family station wagon was piled high with tents, sleeping bags, ice chests, and everything else people need to rough it comfortably in the woods. The Hatchmires headed away from home toward an adventure they never expected.

During the two-day drive, Cathy, the ten-year-old, and Mark, aged thirteen, read books and happily played games like "who can find more cows on my side of the road?" Peter, for most of the trip, sat stubbornly glued against the door, sulking as visibly as possible and every now and then saying something depressing like: "Why can't we do fun things like go to the beach?" or, "They haven't even got a lake to swim in."

After a trip that lasted long enough for Mrs. Hatchmire to fit in three stirring lectures to a captive audience, the station wagon at last lumbered through the entrance to the Yellow River Forest Campground. Within minutes after finding their site, the area was filled with a confused collection of tent poles, sleeping bags, and hiking gear. An hour's hard work, with everyone pitching in (except Peter, of course), turned the chaos into a well-organized camp. When most things were in place, Mr. Hatchmire called a family meeting.

"Now listen carefully," he said in his strictest voice. "No one is allowed to wander off into the woods alone. You must stay in the cleared campsite area and on the marked trails. That's a rule. Do you all understand?"

17

Mark and Cathy studied the area to make sure they recognized the boundaries.

Peter stared at the ground in front of him and grunted. "This will be a swell time. We can sit in front of our tents and do nothing. What a blast."

"Peter." His dad had heard his comment. "The forest ranger warned us that this campground is in the middle of a big, uncivilized forest where dangerous animals have often been spotted. If you go into the woods alone, you could be eaten by a bear."

"I don't think a bear would eat Peter. He'd be too tough to chew," offered Cathy.

After a sneering glance at his sister, Peter simply said, "If I met a bear, at least it would be something exciting."

At every meal, Mrs. Hatchmire assigned jobs to each member of the family. After breakfast on the second day, she asked Peter to pour out the bacon grease in a clump of overgrown weeds near the far edge of the campsite, behind the two tents. Peter, blocked from the view of his family by the tents, stood by the weeds, shifting his weight from one foot to the other, watching the last bit of grease drizzle reluctantly from the can.

Suddenly a rustling in the bushes caught his attention. It seemed to have come from a spot about ten feet into the woods. Peter remembered his father's warning about wild animals and felt a bit frightened. But his curiosity was aroused. He knew the rule against stepping into the wooded area, and hesitated for a minute. Then the rustling noise sounded again.

By now his curiosity was far greater than any mild inclination he had to obey his father. In a nervous whisper to no one, he said, "I really ought to find out what that noise is. I'll check real quick and come right back. Mother and Dad won't even know I went into the woods. And even if they did find out, all I'd get is another stupid sermon from Mother."

After looking quickly to make sure no one in his family was watching, Peter cautiously stepped across the line that divided the campsite from the woods.

About ten minutes passed.

Cathy called out, "Peter, come help dry the dishes."

When Peter failed to appear, Mark shouted, "C'mon Peter. You have to help too. Mom, make Peter do his work."

Still no word from Peter.

After a hurried search in a few obvious hiding places, Mark and Cathy felt alarmed. "Mom, Dad, we can't find Peter."

Mr. and Mrs. Hatchmire, who were lounging comfortably in a double hammock, jumped to the ground and shouted for their missing son. A search of neighboring campsites, the recreation area, and the two nature trails leading into the woods did not turn up Peter. Cathy, while hunting along the outskirts of their campsite in back of the two tents, noticed a few broken branches just behind a clump of weeds that seemed to give off a faint smell like bacon, but she thought nothing of it.

By 10:30 that morning, a trembling, white-faced Mr. Hatchmire was perched on the edge of a cold metal chair in the Yellow River Police Station, doing his best to describe Peter to Sergeant Orville Steubins. Sergeant Steubins, an overweight, balding, gruff-looking man, listened attentively, grunting in his most official tone every five or six seconds.

When Mr. Hatchmire had concluded his description and unhappy narrative of what had happened, Steubins took firm hold of the radio microphone, arranged the dials to permit transmission to the five Yellow River Police patrol cars, to the forest ranger headquarters, and to the state police, then harshly barked, "Missing child; age, nine; name, Peter Hatchmire. Last seen in section *C* of the Yellow River Forest Campground. Description: height, four feet six inches; blond, wavy hair over his ears; thin. Missing since eight thirty this morning. Disappeared into the woods behind Campsite *C*-thirty-four. Wearing dungarees, yellow polo shirt, and sneakers. No evidence as to whereabouts. Call this office with any information you find."

Steubins replaced the mike into the holder, turned to Mr. Hatchmire, and was about to speak when the radio buzzer sounded. The sergeant wheeled around to switch on the receiver, then listened to news from the state police that sent a chill through the entire length of Mr. Hatchmire's back. Marvin Magursky, one of the most ruthless, cruel, tough criminals ever placed behind bars, had escaped from Yellow River County Maximum Security Prison earlier that morning. His breakout was discovered at 6:30 A.M, just two hours before Peter's disappearance. The authorities had no exact knowledge of Magursky's whereabouts, but most were guessing he would hide out in the deep woods of Yellow River Forest.

Steubins's jaw dropped as he listened, together with Mr. Hatchmire, to more bad news. For several months prior to his escape, Magursky had been boasting to the prison guards that he would soon put together an international crime organization that no power on earth would be able to control. It is true, of course, that some people in prison dream of heroic criminal achievements just as little boys sometimes like to pretend they can fly like Superman, but no one regarded Magursky's talk as wishful thinking. He possessed the brains, the muscle, and the connections to make good his boast. One thing he lacked—money. And kidnapping was a cruel but effective means for quickly getting one's hands on a sizeable amount of cash.

The Hatchmires checked into a local motel to wait for word of their son. Just after four o'clock that afternoon, a motorist hurriedly pulled up to the police station, ran quickly inside, and handed a note to Sergeant Steubins.

"Where did you get this?" Steubins demanded before he opened it.

Gasping for breath, the driver of the car panted, "I was driving on Route Eighty-six on the south side of the forest when a man suddenly jumped into the middle of the road and waved for me to stop. He stuck this note in my face and ordered me to take it to the police."

Steubins tore open the envelope. He read the note aloud.

> If you want to see your brat alive, bring $25,000 cash to a log cabin four miles due west of Lake Farragut. Come alone and unarmed at midnight Friday. When I get the money, you get the kid. If I see or hear more than one person, the kid gets killed.
>
> Magursky

Kidnappers do not usually sign their names, but Magursky was different. He craved recognition, even to the point of doing foolish things.

As soon as the motorist left, Fenton Dillow, the FBI agent who had arrived at the police station an hour earlier, plugged into a conference telephone call between the director of the FBI and three top investigators. After Dillow relayed the details of the case to that point, the director assumed leadership.

"Men," the director began, "I don't need to tell you how important it is that we capture Magursky. This case demands top priority. If Magursky escapes with twenty-five thousand in cash, we may not get him for years."

One of the agents responded, "Magursky could build a criminal empire that would make every previous gang look like a church choir."

Another agent spoke up. "We need to assign the best man available to this case."

The third agent added, "I agree. This case requires all-out effort."

"Don't forget a young boy's life is also at stake," the FBI director reminded them. "I want each of you to go over the names of every crime fighter you can think of, then pick the one person in all the world whom you believe can handle this emergency."

After a minute's pause, the director requested some answers. "Well?"

Agent #1: "Captain Al Scabbard."

Agent #2: "Nobody comes close to Captain Scabbard."

Agent #3: "I vote for Agent Joe Broderick. He's specialized in kidnapping cases for over twenty years."

Director: "My choice is Scabbard. That makes it three to one. I'll contact him at once."

It was dinnertime in the Scabbard home on that Thursday evening. The phone call interrupted seven-year-old Billy in the middle of his efforts to persuade his mother never to serve broccoli again. Scabbard smiled as he reached for the phone, watching Billy's contortions as a forkful of broccoli came dangerously close to his offended taste buds.

Sally, Scabbard's attractive wife, who never thought her hair looked quite right, reacted instinctively to the phone call with a stiffened neck and a quick, deep breath. In the Scabbard home, a phone call could be an invitation for Lisa, their sociable thirteen-year-old daughter, to come to a slumber party, or it could be the beginning of another hair-raising, nerve-racking adventure for Captain Scabbard. Sometimes Sally wished that Al would have been just an ordinary man, working from eight to five, watching football on Monday nights, cutting the lawn on Saturday morning, and barbecuing hamburgers on Saturday afternoon. But, "The Lord simply hasn't called my husband to that kind of life," she

24

often reminded herself with a mixture of sadness and excitement.

As she watched Al's smile at Billy lower into a determined frown, Sally knew that this call was not an invitation to a slumber party. Captain Scabbard listened for a few minues, then, before hanging up, said, "I'll call you right back." Captain Al looked thoughtfully at the phone for a moment, then turned to his family and informed them of the dilemma faced by the FBI and the Hatchmire family.

Before anyone responded, the Scabbards joined hands, as was their custom whenever a major problem faced them, and Captain Scabbard led his family in prayer asking God for clear guidance. He then invited each member of the family to express his or her opinion.

Billy was the first to speak. "Boy, if I was kidnapped, I'd sure want you to be the one looking for me. I think you should go."

Lisa followed Billy, speaking softly. Her eyes were glistening with moisture. "Dad, I think God would want you to help. I'll pray for you every day you're gone."

Sally spoke last. "Honey, sometimes it's so hard to watch you go. But for me to complain would be to stand in the way of the Lord's purpose for you. I still feel like complaining, but I'll wait till you get back."

Captain Scabbard leaned over to kiss his wife, hugged his kids, then called the director back to tell him that he would help. A phone call to the airport secured reservations on a plane leaving in a little more than an hour. Scabbard went quickly to the closet to get his well-worn brown leather suitcase, but it was not there.

"Sally," Scabbard called out a bit harshly, "where on earth is my suitcase? I can't find it."

"I don't know where it is," she replied with an edge in her voice. "The last time I saw it, it was in the closet."

"Well, it's not there now," Al stated.

Within seconds, Billy rushed into his dad's bedroom, lugging a brown suitcase. "Here it is, Dad. I was using it to keep my toys in."

"Billy, I've told you before to stay away from my things. This suitcase stays in the closet. Do you understand?" barked Billy's dad.

"Yes, sir," answered Billy, looking away from his angry father.

Captain Scabbard realized at once what he had done. "Billy, I shouldn't have snapped at you." Reaching out to touch his son on the shoulder, Captain Al looked straight into Billy's eyes and said, "Son, I'm sorry. I was wrong. You were wrong to use the suitcase for your toys, and I was wrong for yelling at you."

"Honey," Al called to his wife. "We need another moment of prayer before I go. Will you bring Lisa and join us?"

26

After they prayed together, Billy's eyes were sparkling again as he helped his dad pack for the trip. Within a few minutes, Captain Al Scabbard was on his way to catch the next plane to Yellow River Forest.

The ransom was due midnight Friday. Captain Scabbard walked into the Yellow River Police Station at 11:15 Thursday night. By the time he arrived, there were eighteen people including Mr. Hatchmire crowded into Sergeant Steubins's small outer office. Fenton Dillow, the senior FBI agent, was pointing to a map of the forest showing the precise location of Lake Farragut. Four special agents were attentively following Dillow's geography lesson, along with six blue-uniformed local police and five state police dressed in gray.

Sergeant Steubins was standing with his burly hand on Mr. Hatchmire's shoulder, offering the kind of well-meaning but empty reassurance that usually makes people feel worse.

When the door opened, everyone turned to see who was entering. Captain Scabbard quietly said, "I'm Al Scabbard," and from that moment he was in command, not because he forcibly took over—everyone in the room just knew he should be in charge.

Agent Dillow stepped across the room, elbowing his way past the portly Steubins, to greet the newcomer.

"Captain Scabbard," Dillow said, "I'm glad you're here. I'm Fenton Dillow, FBI. If you'll come over to the map, I'll show you the location of the cabin where the money is to be delivered tomorrow night."

Scabbard smiled courteously but said, "First, I'd like to meet Mr. Hatchmire. Is he here?"

Mr. Hatchmire spoke up brightly. "Yes, I'm Peter's father."

"Sir," Scabbard said slowly, shaking his hand firmly and resting his other hand on Mr. Hatchmire's shoulder. "I want you to know that I will place top priority on returning your son to you."

Somehow, when Captain Scabbard spoke, people sensed a certain power that calmed whatever troubled feelings they had. They received the clear impression that Scabbard did not use words lightly.

Captain Al then asked to meet everyone in the room. Dillow impatiently shook his head, thinking that a round of introductions was a waste of precious time. But long ago, Scabbard had realized that the solutions to most problems were discovered through studying people, not situations. Scabbard turned to Dillow and firmly said, "I want to meet everyone before I do anything else." Dillow agreed.

As Scabbard shook each individual's hand, he intently observed everything about them. One man, Agent Bertram Scampini, failed to look Scabbard straight in the eye as they greeted one another. The Captain made a mental note of that.

When the introductions were over, Scabbard took Dillow into the back office next to the jail cells and asked, "Is there any reason you know why Scampini wouldn't want me here?"

Dillow's eyes opened wide. "Well, when we were deciding who we should ask to help us, Scampini was the only one of the group who picked someone other than you. But how did you know?"

Scabbard ignored Dillow's puzzled question. "Who did Scampini want?" he asked.

"An older agent named Joe Broderick. Broderick's a good man, and he has had a lot of success with kidnap cases, but—well, frankly—he is past his prime. He's just not that sharp anymore. The director has put him out to pasture on more routine cases."

"Call the prison." Scabbard was all business now. He spoke quickly. "Ask the warden for a list of every visitor who came to see Magursky from the first day he was locked up. I also want the names of every person who sent mail to Magursky and those who received mail from Magursky. I'll need that information tomorrow by noon."

Dillow agreed to call the warden but later admitted that he had not the foggiest idea why Scabbard demanded that information. And yet he knew Scabbard's reputation for smelling clues where no one else detected even a faint scent.

Captain Scabbard spent the next two and a half hours studying both the map of the area surrounding the appointed cabin and a police folder of information on Magursky. Scabbard carefully absorbed every detail he read: Magursky was six feet four inches tall, weighed 280, played tackle in a semi-pro football league, had been the wrestling champion in prison every year of his sentence, and had well earned the reputation of a merciless and ruthless criminal.

With that information tucked uncomfortably in his mind, Captain Scabbard found a cot in an empty cell and, at 3:30 in the morning, stretched out for a few hours of badly needed sleep.

Steubins poked his head into Scabbard's cell at 7:00 A.M. Although every bone in his body screamed for more rest, Scabbard quickly rose and dressed. After a miserable breakfast of lukewarm coffee and runny eggs served up by Steubins on his second-hand hot plate, Scabbard huddled with Dillow to plan strategy. By now, the FBI had collected $25,000 in cash from area banks. A team of agents and police worked feverishly for the rest of the day marking each bill for later identification in case Magursky escaped with the money. At 2:00 P.M., a gray-uniformed

30

state policeman interrupted Scabbard's conference with Dillow to hand him a special delivery envelope from the warden of the Yellow River County Maximum Security Prison. Scabbard accepted it gratefully, without mentioning that it was two hours late.

He quickly ripped open the envelope and scanned the enclosed pages listing people who had communicated with Magursky. Halfway down the third page, his eye stopped abruptly on item fifty-six.

> #56: FBI Special Agent Bertram Scampini, assigned to follow-up surveillance of Inmate Magursky, visited Magursky three times: January 24, February 18, March 21.

Scabbard immediately reached for the phone. As soon as the director of the FBI was on the line, Scabbard asked, "Sir, please check your files to see which agent was assigned to follow-up surveillance of Magursky while he was in prison."

In less than a minute, the director answered, "Matthew Hernst had been put on the case but was killed in a car accident early last January. No one had been selected to replace him. Why do you ask?"

"I'll know better tonight how to answer you, sir," Scabbard said. "I'll be in touch. Thank you."

Scabbard leaned back in the swivel chair, folded his hands on his lap, stared straight ahead through narrowly closed eyes, and thought. Whenever his eyes tightened into a narrow slit and his folded hands began slowly wrestling with each other, one could be certain that Scabbard's agile mind was dashing through the obstacle course of clues, false leads, and possible theories on its way to a carefully designed plan for dealing with the problem at hand. I once heard Scabbard deliver a high school graduation speech on the need to think before acting. If I recall correctly, the talk was entitled "We Do What We Think—So Think Carefully."

After spending a good twenty minutes with narrowed eyes and moving hands, Captain Al suddenly rose with the abrupt deliberateness of a man who knew what he had to do and wanted to get on with it.

Dillow had been waiting expectantly for Scabbard to spring into action.

"Call Scampini and the other two agents in here," Captain Scabbard ordered Dillow without explanation.

Agent Banks came in first, then Sattler, and finally Scampini.

Scabbard, with no trace of a smile, got right down to business.

"Men, here's my plan. Magursky is smart and

he's tough. If I go to the cabin alone, I may not be able to rescue Peter and capture Magursky. We have no idea what he might do. He could pull a stunt like loosing a snake in the cabin with Peter tied up, figuring he could escape while I got rid of the snake. We must anticipate some such plan. Two men must go to the cabin. My suggestion is that one of you three go into the cabin with the money. Margusky has no idea that I'm involved in the case. My not appearing shouldn't arouse suspicion. I'll wait outside until the boy is safe. Then I'll get Magursky."

"I'm not sure, Captain Scabbard," Agent Sattler argued. "It sounds too risky. Magursky said he'd kill the boy if he saw any hint that a second person had come. I'd rather take our chances with one man."

Scabbard's brow furrowed into a look of impatience. After carefully thinking through a plan and studying every option, he was in no mood for debate. One of his recurring struggles, and one that almost cost him his life in an incident I may tell you about later, was his tendency to be so sure of himself that he would not consider someone else's viewpoint. Scabbard felt like exploding at Sattler, but, making a definite choice to do what was right, he forced his mouth to say, "I agree with you, Sattler, that my plan includes a definite risk. What do you suggest?"

"Well," began Sattler, "no one could handle a giant like Magursky except you. I vote to ask you to go it alone."

"I appreciate your confidence in me, although I feel it's rather badly overstated. What do the rest of you think?" asked Scabbard.

Of the other three (Dillow, Banks, and Scampini), only Scampini agreed with Sattler, and he expressed his opinion rather forcefully. Dillow and Banks supported Scabbard's plan for sending two men instead of one.

"Then it is decided by a vote of three to two," announced Scabbard. "We'll send two men on the job. Any one of you could handle the assignment effectively, but my choice is Scampini. He's tough, quick, and dependable. Any objections?"

Captain Al had maneuvered the conversation to avoid any opposition. Dillow of course was aware that Scabbard selected Scampini for good reason, although he had not the vaguest notion what the reason was. Banks and Sattler were only too willing to applaud Scabbard's choice. Even FBI men occasionally prefer remaining at a distance from front-line battles, particularly when a head-on collision with a man like Magursky is involved. And Scampini could not refuse the assignment without either arousing suspicion or playing the part of a coward.

Later that evening, a little past 10:00, Captain

Scabbard and Bertram Scampini climbed into a jeep, Scabbard armed with a knife and pistol, and Scampini, as instructed by the ransom note, completely unarmed. A briefcase bulging with $25,000 in marked bills was carefully positioned on the floor under the driver's seat. Scabbard's hands were steady as he grasped the steering wheel. His thick, dark eyebrows pressed down over his piercing eyes, signaling that Scabbard was intense, ready for action. Climbing into the jeep, Agent Scampini tripped and spilled a thermos of coffee on his shirt. By the time the coffee had dried, his body was drenched with nervous perspiration despite the cool mountain air.

By 10:35 P.M., the jeep pulled within sight of Lake Farragut. Everything was still. The full moon cast dark shadows of tall pines on the motionless lake. An eerie silence was broken only by the sound of a bird flying through the branches far above the ground.

"OK, let's move," whispered Scabbard. "The cabin should be less than an hour's walk if we keep to a slow, careful pace. There's the path off to the left. Magursky may be watching the trail to see if you're alone. You go on ahead. I'll follow close behind."

Scampini turned in the direction Scabbard pointed and could see nothing but darkness. The full, thickly spreading trees formed a huge umbrella over the entire woods, blocking the moon from providing any light for the trail. Hesitantly, with his flashlight guiding his way, Scampini moved into the woods. Scabbard had already taken to the dense underbrush to the left of the trail. He waited for Scampini to get going, then followed noiselessly like a panther tracking its prey, keeping a distance of about thirty feet behind the frightened agent.

They had been walking for nearly twenty minutes when suddenly Scabbard heard a shrill, piercing cry. It was Scampini. Leaping to the path, Scabbard shone his flashlight on a small, ferocious bear, its white fangs glistening in the light, poised menacingly over a fallen Scampini.

From his distance of thirty feet, Scabbard hurled his hunting knife toward the savage beast. The blade found its mark, sinking deeply into the bear's neck. Within seconds, Scabbard tackled the thickly muscled bear with a force that knocked it abruptly to the ground. He ducked a deadly swing of the bear's sharp-clawed paw, yanked his knife from the bloody wound, and thrust it solidly into its chest.

The bear roared, then collapsed with a heavy thud beside the frozen FBI agent.

"Are you all right?" asked Scabbard, helping the trembling Scampini to his feet.

"Is—is it dead?" stuttered Scampini.

"Yes. Where are you hurt? Let me look."

Scampini was terrified but unhurt (except for a few small scratches) and reluctantly, at Scabbard's insistence, got up and resumed his lonely trek toward the cabin. Scabbard started to follow, then turned back briefly to the fallen bear to add a new wrinkle to his strategy.

At 11:40, twenty minutes before the meeting with Magursky was scheduled to occur, the cabin in the woods came into view. It was small, poorly built and rundown, the sort of cabin a strange old hermit would call home. A rickety wooden door, held onto the front wall with huge, rusty metal hinges, was closed tightly. Scabbard quickly circled the cabin. The other three sides had one window apiece, each protected with thin iron bars on the outside of the cracked glass.

Every muscle in Captain Scabbard's body was tense, ready to spring into quick action. He moved quietly. One sound hinting that two men had come, and Peter Hatchmire would never have the opportunity to disobey his parents again.

Scabbard hooted an owl call, the prearranged signal for Scampini to proceed to the door, then silently crept up to the window on the north side of the cabin.

Scambini's trembling fist knocked twice. It was one minute before midnight.

"You better be alone," a mean voice bellowed

from inside. "I got a gun aimed right at this kid's head. Come in slow with both hands in front of you."

Nervously clutching the briefcase full of money, Scampini pushed open the heavy door. The scratchy sound of the rusty hinges stubbornly yielding to force sent a cold shiver through Scampini's body.

Scabbard risked a peek into the window. Magursky was standing in the center of the one room, bigger and tougher-looking than even Captain Scabbard had anticipated. Peter, tied securely with coarse rope, stood right in front of Magursky with the barrel of a .38 pistol lodged against his forehead.

As soon as Scampini's face appeared from behind the door, Magursky's eyes opened wide. "What in tarnation are *you* doing here?" he barked. "Are you pulling some sort of double cross? If you are, say goodbye to this world."

Scampini turned white. In a weak, shaky voice, he said, "Look, I volunteered for this job to make sure that you didn't get captured. Give me the kid and you escape with the money."

Magursky peered at Scampini, then grabbed the boy and shouted, "All right, whoever else is out there, get in here now or the kid gets it."

Scabbard had thought ahead. He guessed that perhaps the bear that he had killed earlier that night might prove useful to him, and he had dragged it with him all the way. As soon as Scampini had disappeared into the cabin, Scabbard had propped the bear up against the door. When Magursky shouted, Scabbard released the door latch. The weight of the beast pushed the door open slowly. The hinges sang their awful tune, winning Magursky's full attention. Scabbard dashed back to the window in time to see the door suddenly swing wide open and the ferocious-looking bear sprawl right in front of Magursky.

The moment it took Magursky to realize the bear was dead was enough time for Scabbard to rip the iron bars from the window and hurl his body through the glass.

With one lightning move, he threw Peter out of the way and sent a crunching blow to Magursky's jaw. Magursky reeled backward, dropping his gun. Scampini grabbed the weapon and shouted, "Freeze."

Magursky, rubbing a jaw that felt like a sledgehammer had just landed on it, said, "Attaboy, Bert. Let's kill these two and split."

Scabbard's mind raced.

"Scampini," he said firmly, "it's no secret that you're in with Magursky. I checked to see who visited him in prison, and without official reason you were there three times. I picked you for this job to expose your connection with Magursky."

"No way, Scabbard. You're bluffing," stammered Scampini. "FBI agents visit prisoners all the time, looking for information. Dillow knows nothing. I'll kill you and tell the FBI you were shot by Magursky when he heard you outside the cabin. Magursky, take the money. I'll kill Scabbard and the kid. Our plans are still good. I can still be your inside man in the FBI."

Scabbard, looking calm but determined, spoke up. "Magursky, do you want somebody as nervous as Scampini working for you? Look at him. He's shaking like a teenage kid before his first date. Some criminal empire you'll build with flimsy material like that."

"Don't listen to him, Magursky," squealed Scampini in a higher-pitched voice than before. He was trembling with nervousness. Scabbard struck. How a man can move six feet across a room in less time than it takes a nervous man to pull a trigger, I don't really know. If I told you Tony Cannon had done it, you would of course not be surprised. But Scabbard somehow managed it. His right hand grabbed the pistol from Scampini, and his left delivered a staggering blow into Scampini's midriff.

When you have been hit by Captain Al Scabbard, especially in the stomach, there is only one thing you can do. And Scampini did it—he slumped to the floor in a helpless heap.

By this time Magursky had recovered enough from his encounter with Scabbard's fist to move toward the captain. Peter, still with his hands tied tightly, ran across the room and kicked Magursky in the shin with all the strength his nine-year-old body could muster. The blow was not much, but it startled Magursky enough to give Scabbard time to swing around and point the pistol straight at Magursky.

"OK, that's far enough. Another step and you'll walk into a bullet."

Scabbard pulled his two-way radio from his belt holder and called for the state police helicopter.

Scabbard then herded Scampini and Magursky into the northwest corner of the cabin. Scabbard untied Peter, made sure he was OK, and informed him that if his last name were Scabbard, he would be in for one solid spanking for breaking the rule about wandering off from the campsite. He ordered Peter to stand behind him. While they waited for the police to arrive, Scabbard played back his earlier conversation with Scampini, which he had recorded on the miniature tape recorder tucked inside his wrist watch. Scampini, still clutching his bruised stomach, listened to his own voice admit criminal association with Magursky.

By 2:30 Saturday morning, Magursky and Scampini were locked as securely as anyone could be in Steubins's jail, under heavy guard, waiting for the prison van to transport them to the penitentiary. The $25,000 was sealed in Steubins's small office safe until it could be returned to the banks. And Peter was returned to his family.

Mr. Hatchmire was the first to reach his son. After a tearful embrace with his dad, Peter was passed around from his mother to his brother and sister for tight hugs and warm kisses. And then, just as Mr. Hatchmire was about to follow Captain Scabbard's advice to paddle his foolish son, Mrs. Hatchmire stepped in between Peter and his dad, took Peter firmly by the shoulder, and launched into a long lecture on the evil of disobedience. Mark and Cathy smiled when they saw Peter, in the middle of his mother's speech, turn his head and utter under his breath, "At least Magursky didn't preach any sermons." Captain Scabbard shook his head and walked away.

2

Iron Ike's
Four Death Plans

The adventure you are about to read may "tax your credulity" as Professor Bill Perriwinkle might say. You have not been introduced to the good professor yet, but because you will hear about him a little in this adventure and quite a bit in a few later ones, it might be good if I took the time to briefly introduce him to you now.

Professor William Lemuel Perriwinkle III was a college instructor. He taught English literature and philosophy at Cornwell University, where he had earlier earned his doctor's degree at the age of twenty-two. Although most students liked and respected Perriwinkle, they could not help but chuckle when he entered a classroom or rode his bicycle across campus. He really did look a little bit funny. He stood just under five feet ten inches tall in his stocking feet, which usually had a big toe sticking through a hole in each sock. (Everyone knew about it, because Perriwinkle was in the habit of removing his shoes whenever he sat at a desk studying in the library. You could tell when he found something exciting in his reading. Both big toes would furiously move up and down, making the holes in his socks bigger than before.)

The professor was exceptionally thin. One of his students claimed that he was so skinny that he had to move about in the shower to get wet. If you are getting the picture, you have already guessed that Perriwinkle wore dark, thick-framed glasses that were usually perched halfway down his narrow, pointed, and rather prominent nose. His medium brown hair either refused to cooperate with a comb or else never met one, and his clothing looked like a style that was out of date twenty years ago.

The thing that stood out the most about Perriwinkle was his huge vocabulary. Rumor had it that his big toes first began their excited, sock-ripping pounding when his parents gave him a thick, college-level dictionary for his seventh birthday. Even Scabbard, who first met the professor when he took an evening course in modern philosophy, had a hard time understanding him. Scabbard told me about the time in class when he asked Dr. Perriwinkle why some people seemed to drift naturally toward a life of crime with no interference from their consciences. Naturally he expected to hear something about man's sinful nature, which is concerned more with feeling good than with doing right, but Perriwinkle's answer made Scabbard blink in confusion. As near as I can recall, the professor said: "The enigma you have identified reduces ultimately to the question of whether the genesis of the criminal aberration is fundamentally ontological, volitional, or relational."

Well, enough about Perriwinkle. Perhaps you have a good idea of what he was like, one that you'll remember when you meet him later on.

Let's get on now with this adventure, in which Captain Scabbard and Archie Cramer (who couldn't have been more unlike Professor Perriwinkle) teamed up to put behind bars an elite, ruthless band of criminals headed up by Isaac "Ike" Watson, known in international police circles as "Iron Ike."

Before I wrote any of these adventures, I always discussed them with Scabbard. When I went to his house with the adventure of Iron Ike on my mind, I found Scabbard in an unusually relaxed mood. He greeted me at the door with a big smile and said, "C'mon in. Have a seat." After we were settled in two comfortable chairs, Scabbard very warmly asked, "Now, which adventure do you want to discuss today?" Without any idea that Scabbard would react as he did, I simply said, "I'm putting together the story on Iron Ike Watson."

As soon as he heard that name, Captain Scabbard visibly stiffened. He grasped the solid oak arms of his chair so tightly that his fingers left an imprint in the wood. I remember feeling at the time that I'd rather face ten hungry lions than Al Scabbard when he was like that. With a look so intense that I could almost feel the heat, he slowly and with an awful mixture of dread and disgust in his voice said, "The man had no conscience."

For a moment I sat there nervously, a little puzzled. I was not sure why the memory of a man without a conscience triggered such a strong reaction in Scabbard. You can probably remember a number of times when life would have been far more comfortable if a nagging conscience would have quieted down—like the time the teacher passed out a test for which you had not studied, and the smartest girl in the class was sitting right next to you, putting down answers that just a slight sideways glance would have enabled you to see.

Or perhaps the time you needed just one more dollar to buy the pocketknife upon which your eternal happiness seemed to depend, and there, on

Dad's dresser, was a lone dollar bill begging to be picked up and put into your pocket. Maybe you can recall how your conscience fought you, insisting that you do what was right no matter how much you wanted to do wrong. It even argued back when you tried to convince yourself that God had made your dad leave the dollar there to provide you with what you wanted. "After all," you probably said to yourself, "doesn't God want me to be happy?"

At times like that, it's pretty hard to think of your conscience as a friend whom you want to know better. But after Scabbard explained to me that a dead conscience was responsible for what Iron Ike was like, I found myself sensing a new respect and appreciation for my conscience.

When Scabbard had relaxed enough to go on, he filled in the details of the adventure of Iron Ike.

The story began on a Thursday afternoon in the secret penthouse headquarters of Isaac "Iron Ike" Watson. Around a large, rectangular, brightly polished conference table sat twelve of the most skilled killers in all the world, handpicked by Iron Ike himself for "Operation Two."

At 2:30 sharp, Ike called the meeting to order. In his cold, unemotional, smooth but ruthless style, which had earned him the nickname "Iron Ike," he began.

"Gentlemen, I have just signed a contract with

the Baron, who will pay us twelve million dollars to permanently eliminate two men—the vice-president of the United States and Captain Al Scabbard."

He waited a moment to let his words penetrate into the hardened men seated before him.

Fritz Varillio, who of all the men in the room enjoyed his work the most, spoke quickly. "The vice-president should be no problem. But Scabbard—that's another matter."

Seated across from Fritz, Sharkey Paxton shook his head. "Ike, our competitors have tried to ice Scabbard a dozen times. He's smart. We'll need a foolproof plan."

Iron Ike's lips curled into a cold smile as he pulled out a folder marked "Operation Two."

"Gentlemen, get out your notebooks. Listen carefully as I describe Operation Two. Within three weeks, two men will be dead if you follow every detail of my plan. Each of you will receive six hundred thousand dollars. The one who kills the vice-president gets an extra six hundred thousand. Whoever kills Scabbard gets two million. I take the rest. There must be no mistakes. I want the vice-president dead because I want the money. I want Scabbard dead because I hate him."

At 5:15 P.M., two hours and forty-five minutes after the conference had begun, twelve deadly killers left Iron Ike's headquarters with a carefully-thought-through plan to kill the vice-president of the United States and Captain Al Scabbard. Iron Ike remained seated in his chair at the head of the large deserted table, slowly rubbing his hands together, feeling an evil pleasure at the thought of attending Al Scabbard's funeral.

Two days before the penthouse meeting had taken place, Al Scabbard received a special delivery letter from the office of the vice-president of the United States. It was all that his wife, Sally, could do to keep from opening it before her husband returned home. When he walked in the door at ten minutes till six, Sally ran to him waving the letter.

"Al, Al! A letter from our vice-president. Open it. See what it says! Quick."

His kids, Lisa and Billy, were right behind their mother, jumping up and down with excitement.

"OK, OK," Al said, feeling just as eager as his family. When he had carefully torn open the envelope, he read the letter aloud:

OF THE UNITED STATES OF AMERICA

Dear Captain Scabbard,

In recognition of your dedication both to the cause of justice and to the principles of Christianity, which has been an example to so many of our people, you have been chosen to receive the Vice-President's Annual Citizen of the Year Award. You are hereby invited to a banquet to be held in your honor at the White House on October 17 at 7 P.M. On that occasion, you will be recognized as the recipient of this award, which carries with it a $10,000 check. I will be honored to preside at the banquet.

Sincerely,

George D. Hartley

George D. Hartley
Vice-president of the United States

Please R.S.V.P. by phone to my office upon receipt of this letter.

When Al finished reading the letter, all four Scabbards stood quietly in the hallway for about five seconds. Then Sally wrapped her arms around her husband and said, "Oh, honey, I'm so proud of you."

Lisa squeezed in next to her mother and hugged her daddy around the waist. Billy said, "Hey, do we get to go? Wow, I hope so. Dinner at the White House. Wait till I tell my friends."

After a few hectic minutes of kisses, exclamations, and other happy noises, Sally suddenly put her hands to her face and shrieked, "Oh, no, the lamb chops!"

She flew into the kitchen, pushing her way through smoke to see burned lamb chops sizzling under the broiler. "Oh, Al, they're burned to a crisp," she wailed.

Captain Scabbard cheerfully walked over to his distraught wife, put his arm on her shoulder, and said, "Honey, with an unexpected ten thousand coming our way in three weeks, I think I can afford to take you out to dinner tonight. Put on your dressiest dress, and I'll take you to the best restaurant in town. Kids, hurry up and get ready. Tonight's a night to celebrate."

Sally disposed of the lamb chops, then went to her bedroom to get ready. As she took her favorite dress from the closet, an unwelcome thought intruded into her mind. She tried to push it back, but she could not help wondering if her husband was not letting himself feel a little proud. Since he had read the letter twenty minutes ago, he had not mentioned the Lord at all. Usually the first thing he did when unexpected news came was to express thanks if the news was good and pray for strength if it was bad. *Well, maybe he thanked the Lord to himself. And after all, I guess he does have a right to feel pretty good,* Sally thought to herself.

As Captain Al and his family happily packed into their car and went off to enjoy a big dinner, none of them even dreamed that Iron Ike Watson had heard about the award four days earlier from his informant in Washington and had planned to complete Operation Two at the award dinner. For the next three weeks, while the Scabbards made preparations for their trip to the nation's capital, Ike's twelve killers systematically followed their detailed instructions to get ready for murdering Al Scabbard and Vice-president Hartley the evening of the banquet.

The genius of Ike's strategy was to come up with four separate foolproof plans to successfully carry out his fiendish intentions. Iron Ike knew of Scabbard's uncanny ability to sense when something out of the ordinary was brewing, but he figured that even Scabbard would not be able to anticipate and stop four different death plans. Operation Two seemed certain to succeed.

Three of Ike's men, including Fritz Varillio, were assigned the job of getting into the kitchen before the banquet to generously sprinkle the dinners intended for Hartley and Scabbard with a deadly poison. Four others were instructed to get hold of the bronze plaque to be awarded Scabbard and to place a delicate wiring system between its cover plate and its backpiece. A remote control mechanism would charge the plaque with 1000 volts at the moment both Hartley and Scabbard were touching it as it was presented to Scabbard.

Sharkey Paxton, killer number eight, was to counterfeit a newspaper photographer's pass to gain entrance to the banquet. His first job was to press the button on the remote control electrical unit to fry the two victims. In the unlikely event that plan failed, he was to come to the dinner equipped with a special camera that quietly fired a lethal poison dart when the shutter was pressed. The dart was so small that when it hit it would penetrate the skin causing a sensation like the bite of a small insect. Within minutes, the victims would be dead.

Operation Two included one last strategy. If all the previous plans were somehow thwarted, three of the remaining four killers were to break into the dining hall and cause a ruckus on the east side of the room to draw attention away from the head table. The twelfth assassin, instructed to secure the credentials of a White House guide, would be stationed on the west side of the room, to the left of the head table. Two shots from a silencer-equipped gun, and a quick exit out the west door, and Operation Two would be over.

Did you ever read the story of the Red Sea's dividing and wonder if it really happened? Well, when I tell you what took place the evening of the banquet, you will either accuse me of writing fairy tales or you will realize that something supernatural took place. If I had not personally talked to several people who were there that evening, I might not have believed it either.

Preparations for Iron Ike's plans went smoothly. Each of his killers did their jobs well. Three of them had managed to gain entrance to the White House kitchen, one as an assistant waiter, one as a deliveryman, and the third as a federal food inspector. Four of the gang had broken into the shop where the plaque was being fashioned and had spent an entire night carefully wiring it with the remote discharge unit. They gave the simple push-button unit to Sharkey Paxton, who had secured his phony pass as a press photographer. He had flown to San Francisco to pick up the specially made dart-firing camera and had spent hours practicing his aim until he was almost as good a shot as Bob Culpepper.

Killers numbers nine, ten, and eleven had devised a plan to break through the security police stationed outside the dining hall, and killer number twelve had kidnapped a White House guide and stolen his credentials. He was ready to stand by the west door, prepared to shoot Hartley and Scabbard in the event his services were needed.

The morning of October 17 found Captain Al Scabbard, his wife, and two children excitedly boarding a plane for their trip to the White House. Billy pressed his face against the window to watch the ground move away, and Lisa, feeling very grown up, asked the stewardess for a copy of *Ladies' Home Journal*.

Al and Sally sat across the aisle from their children. As soon as they were belted into their seats, Al began to talk about the money he would soon receive. "Honey, let's put two thousand dollars in our savings and spend the rest. We could afford a trip to Hawaii and maybe a new car. And you've been wanting new carpeting in our den. Or maybe—"

Sally squirmed a bit, feeling very much like she had felt a few weeks ago after the lamb chops had burned. But now she could not dismiss her worries as easily as she had then. She decided to share her concerns with her husband.

"Al," she hesitantly began, "I think I'm a little worried. It seems like we're accepting all the credit for this award. We haven't even thanked the

Lord for what's happening, and I wonder if we're taking kind of a selfish attitude toward the money."

Even men like Al Scabbard sometimes get caught in the grip of sin. Al turned to his wife and said rather sharply, "Look, Sally, can't you just accept me without giving me a lecture on being spiritual? I know God's behind this and I'm grateful. But for crying out loud, isn't it all right to just enjoy what you get sometimes? Honestly, Sally, sometimes I wonder if your strict upbringing didn't make you a legalist."

Sally turned away and softly said, "OK, honey." Al told me later that he was aware of a miserable pressure building up inside of him, but he just could not seem to find the right valve to let it go.

For the rest of the flight, Billy stared out the window, which framed rolling plains of pure white clouds. Lisa busily studied an article on the proper application of eye makeup, and Sally and Al sat together in uncomfortable silence, broken only once when Al muttered something about the bitter, lukewarm coffee that accompanied his meal.

When the plane landed, Al and Sally were able to rearrange their faces into warm smiles to greet the government dignitary sent to escort them to the White House. After a short ride in an elegant

57

limousine, the four Scabbards were welcomed to the White House by Vice-president Hartley.

As they entered the plush banquet room a few minutes before seven, the entire group of seventy specially invited guests, who had arrived earlier to be there for the Scabbards' entrance, rose to greet the Scabbard family with a warm and almost embarrassingly prolonged round of applause. Sally overheard one older lady turn to the person next to her and say, "He looks like an ordinary man. From what I've heard about him I almost expected him to shine like the sun."

Scabbard was happily surprised to see two of his best friends, Professor Bill Perriwinkle and Archie Cramer, seated at the head table. After enthusiastic handshakes and several emotional embraces, the Scabbards were seated. Lloyd Fetter, Al's Sunday school teacher when he was a boy and the man who had led Al to Christ, was invited to offer thanks for the meal. During his prayer, his warm comments about Al's spiritual growth made Scabbard feel a little unpleasantly warm, much like how you feel when you sit too close to a fire.

Then the vice-president introduced Professor Bill Perriwinkle to offer a few personal words about the guest of honor. With much help from a dictionary, I copied out his words from a tape recording of the banquet that Scabbard loaned me. The first few sentences went like this:

"I am privileged to offer a few simple comments regarding my friendship with Captain Al Scabbard. It is incontrovertibly true that the epistemic foundation of deep relationship of necessity transcends, without of course negating, objective analysis. Logical processes alone are insufficient to explain the ineffably profound amatory bonds which unite people who share a mututal commitment. Mere propositional language could never express character . . ."

I have always wondered if for some reason Perriwinkle enjoyed confusing people. If he did, then his pleasure was rich that evening because no one knew what he was talking about. But everyone safely assumed that he was saying nice things about Scabbard.

While Perriwinkle continued to recite the dictionary, Scabbard, who rarely failed to notice anything even mildly suspicious, observed that everyone in the room wore amused expressions of happy confusion in response to the professor's string of big words; everyone, that is, except two men. A press photographer standing in the rear of the room, holding a rather unusually shaped camera, and a squarely built, unfriendly-looking White House guide standing by the west door had not smiled once. With his attention directed to those two men, Scabbard noted that they exchanged one or two quick glances.

Captain Al Scabbard's mind went into high gear. He figured that something was wrong and that those two men were involved. After Perriwinkle had exhausted the English language and returned to his seat, Scabbard, just before dinner was served, quietly left his seat and walked over to Archie Cramer. In a whisper that no one else could hear, Al said, "Archie, keep your eyes open for trouble. The cameraman in the back and the guide by the west door might be up to something that's not on the program. Stay alert."

When Scabbard had returned to his seat, a stream of waiters emerged from the kitchen carrying three, sometimes four, dinners each. The first man out of the kitchen, however, was holding only two plates. He walked directly to the head table and placed the two dinners in front of Scabbard and Hartley. Captain Scabbard wondered why the rules of etiquette were ignored and he was served before his wife. When his waiter did not return immediately to the kitchen for more dinners, Scabbard quickly guessed what was happening.

As the vice-president innocently plunged his fork into the mashed potatoes, Scabbard went into action. He clumsily reached for the salt and pepper and managed to knock over his water glass at an angle that drenched the vice-president's entire meal. As he got up to help the startled vice-president, he tipped his wife's water glass onto his own meal. With great apologies and well-acted embarrassment, he motioned to another waiter, who was carrying four dinners, to replace the two ruined meals. A quick glance at the photographer revealed what looked like an expression of disgusted frustration.

Sally Scabbard knew that although it was not unusual for her husband to eat his salad with his dinner fork, he was not clumsy. Sensing that something strange was going on, she silently whispered a prayer. "Lord, my husband may be in danger. I know he isn't in close fellowship with You right now, but please protect him anyway."

The rest of the meal went smoothly, except for a not-completely-dry tablecloth that occasionally dripped onto the vice-president's trousers. As soon as everyone had finished the delicious dessert of baked Alaska, Vice-president Hartley, with slightly damp pants, rose to begin the award ceremony. During his introductory comments about the history and significance of the award, Captain Scabbard kept an alert eye on the photographer and the guide. Neither had moved an inch the entire meal. But, when Hartley bent down to pick up the award plaque from under the speaker's rostrum, Scabbard noticed that the photographer, holding his camera with his right hand, slowly but deliberately put his left hand in his suit coat pocket.

Scabbard's mind, which had remained in gear, was racing to determine the connection between Hartley's reaching for the plaque and the photographer's hand now in his left coat pocket. His thoughts were interrupted when the vice-president announced that before awarding the plaque, he would present Scabbard the check for $10,000. Scabbard's attention instantly turned to visions of trips, cars, and a new, larger total in his savings account. With the check securely in his grip, and thoroughly filling his mind, Scabbard failed to observe the anxious, cruel grin that spread across the photographer's face as Hartley extended the plaque toward Scabbard's waiting hand.

At the precise moment the plaque was held by both Hartley and Scabbard, the phony photographer depressed the white button on the small wallet-sized instrument in his pocket.

But nothing happened. The killer pressed the button again, this time harder. Still nothing. His finger still pressing down on the button, he heard Hartley apologize to Scabbard for the small discoloration on the underside of the plaque. The vice-president explained that earlier that afternoon the delivery man had dropped it on the driveway after unwrapping it in his truck to carry it into the dining room.

While the vice-president explained the almost imperceptible blemish, Scabbard noticed that one of the tiny screws holding the face of the plaque onto its bronze backpiece was loose. Looking more closely he could see a very fine wire wrapped around the loose screw. Holding the plaque behind the rostrum so the guests could not see what he was doing, Scabbard deftly removed the screw with his fingernail while the vice-president continued to speak. After the one screw was removed, Scabbard could pry the face of the plaque from the backpiece enough to see the complex maze of delicate wiring inside. With his mind back in top speed, he instantly fitted together the pieces of the puzzle. When the plaque was dropped, the deadly shock mechanism had been jarred enough to short-circuit the current.

Scabbard looked up in time to see the photographer walking toward the head table, holding his camera to his eye. Archie Cramer was already half out of his chair when Scabbard suddenly cried out, ''Archie, get the camera!''

Before the killer could react, Cramer had leaped over the table and snatched the camera away from him. Instinctively the fake photographer delivered to Cramer's jaw a blow powerful enough to crack a solid wooden door. Archie fell back a half step, rubbed his jaw the way you would if somebody had tickled you with a feather, and smiled at the crook. ''Is that the best you can do?'' he asked.

Scabbard spoke quickly. "Archie, reach into his left coat pocket. Bring me whatever is in there." Archie pulled out a small black box with a pushed-in white button and gave it to Scabbard.

A vise-like grip on the killer's shoulder was enough to keep him still until the security police had handcuffed him and led him away.

Archie opened the camera and gave it to Captain Scabbard, who showed Vice-president Hartley the dart-firing pistol inside. Hartley turned white. Scabbard went to the microphone to assure the guests that everything was under control. When the vice-president regained his color, he walked slowly back to the rostrum and concluded the award ceremony.

When he finished his remarks, he asked Professor Perriwinkle to step forward to offer the benediction. Perriwinkle had barely begun, "Omnipotent, immutable Father . . ." when stage four of Operation Two was violently set in motion. Three of Iron Ike's killers broke suddenly into the dining hall through the east door, yelling at the top of their lungs and punching everyone in sight.

Scabbard smiled briefly to himself when he saw Archie race toward the rowdies, knowing that in a few moments all three men would be lying unconscious on the floor. Suddenly he remembered the guide standing at the west door. He turned in time to look straight into the barrel of a pistol aimed directly at his head. With a movement that would have made a magician's hands seem slow, Scabbard grabbed the crystal pepper shaker on the table in front of him and in the same motion hurled it at the killer. Before the killer had time to pull the trigger, the shaker found its mark smack on the tip of the phony guide's nose. The bullet from the gun lodged itself harmlessly in the ceiling above Scabbard's head. The newspaper account of the incident stated that the pepper shaker thrown by Scabbard seemed to move more quickly through the air than the bullet fired by the killer.

Scabbard by this time had raced over and disarmed the last of Iron Ike's band of twelve. Cramer had easily subdued the other three killers as Scabbard had known he would. All three had run headlong into an Archie Cramer fist.

It was at least twenty minutes before the police had removed the criminals and order had been restored. Scabbard had given directions to apprehend the waiter who had carried the two dinners. (I should mention that when the police laid hands on him, he swore that he would not take the rap alone and freely told the police where to find the other two men who had been part of the first stage of Operation Two.)

When all had regained their seats and were relatively calm, Captain Scabbard walked to the speaker's rostrum, cleared his throat, and spoke very softly. No one made a sound. All eyes were fixed on Captain Scabbard.

"Ladies and gentlemen, I must speak to you briefly at the end of this tragically eventful evening. I am of course deeply honored by the award that you have given me. However, I would not be able to sleep tonight if I did not set a few things straight." The "valve" he could not locate earlier was wide open. All the pressure that had built up over the past three weeks, and that had tripled during the plane ride to Washington, was now evaporating quickly into the air. Scabbard continued.

"From the first moment that I learned that I was to be honored with this award, I became preoccupied with the prospect of receiving ten thousand dollars. My attitude was selfish. I foolishly thought that the money was mine to spend as I desired. As we flew to Washington this afternoon, my wife gently and lovingly tried to point out my wrong attitude."

Scabbard turned to his wife and, with moist eyes, said, "Honey, I apologize for treating you unkindly. I was wrong. You were right. Thank you for caring enough to risk my hurting you."

Turning back to the guests, he continued. "My mind was so filled with thoughts of the money that I failed to notice that the plaque that was presented to me had been wired. The little black box that my good friend Archie Cramer removed from the photographer's pocket was a remote control unit, which could charge the plaque with an electrical current strong enough to kill both our vice-president and myself. Had I not been so in love with the money I was about to receive, I would likely have been aware of what was happening. Their plan to kill us didn't work because the mechanism was shortcircuited in the fall Vice-president Hartley has already mentioned. Some will say we were lucky. I believe that the hand of God saved us from death.

"The only cure I know for greed is giving. I therefore would like to announce that I intend to donate the entire amount of ten thousand dollars to the work of foreign missions.

"Again, thank you for this award. Above all, I thank my Savior for continued evidence of His faithfulness to me."

As the audience stood spontaneously to give Captain Scabbard a loud ovation, Sally Scabbard, with mascara-stained tears working their way down her face, removed the last trace of tension between herself and her humbled husband with the kind of embrace usually reserved for newlyweds. After what seemed like hours of pumping handshakes, tearful embraces, and fond farewells, a tired but happy group of four Scabbards managed to exit to a waiting limousine. Lisa, looking up at her still wet-eyed mother, said, "Don't worry, Mom. I know how to fix your eye makeup for you."

The morning after the banquet, newspaper headlines across the nation told the unbelievable story of what had happened. Iron Ike had eagerly purchased the morning edition, expecting to read of the murder of Vice-president Hartley and Captain Al Scabbard. When he read that twelve well-known killers had been captured and that neither Hartley nor Scabbard was even hurt, he crumpled the paper angrily and threw it on the floor.

Archie Cramer had persuaded one of the twelve killers to name the mastermind behind Operation Two. When the police arrived at Iron Ike's penthouse later that morning, they found him lying dead, sprawled out on the thick plush carpeting in the middle of his living room. The police could find no clues to identify either the murderer or the motivation for murder. When Captain Scabbard learned of Iron Ike's mysterious death, he quietly murmured to himself, "Could it be the Baron?"

3

The Baron's Code

As I was studying Captain Scabbard's remarkable life in preparation for this book, I happened to run into an old high school buddy, Larry Davis, who was just as interested in Scabbard as I was. He told me that he had met Al Scabbard about three years earlier. It was through Captain Al's humble attitude and desire to help others that my friend was led to accept Christ as his Savior. Since then he has been investigating the life of the man who led him to the Lord.

When I told him I was writing a book about Scabbard's adventures, he nearly jumped with excitement.

"Hey, I'm a newspaper reporter. Let me write up some of the adventures I've researched. It would be a real pleasure to have a part in telling the world how God has used a man who really gave everything he had to the Lord."

Naturally, I agreed. The following story is written by my friend Larry Davis.

Did you ever wonder what it would be like to have all of Captain Scabbard's friends together at one time? Well, not all of them, because Captain Scabbard has friends all over the country—in fact you might truly say, all over the world. I was really thinking of those friends you and I have come to know so well.

First, Professor William Lemuel Perriwinkle III. Let's just call him Bill. Some folks laugh at him because he's so thin, wears thick glasses, and isn't much of an athlete. (Don't challenge him at checkers or chess, though; I don't think anyone has ever beaten him.) The truth is, Bill is a *brain*. Where there's heavy thinking to be done, Bill is your man. Captain Scabbard knows that and has often called on Bill for help with some of the many problems he is called on to solve.

Remember Archie Cramer? You would if he ever caught you with one of those big fists. He's big and easygoing, but I'll never forget something that happened about three years ago. Captain Scabbard had been in an accident. He was recovering but could only move very slowly and was under doctor's orders to take it easy. Somehow a character known as Rusty, who had it in for Captain Scabbard found out about his condition and figured it was a good chance to get even.

The Captain was resting under a tree on his front lawn when Rusty came by, overturned the chair in which Scabbard was sitting, and then stood by laughing as Captain Scabbard tried to get up. Captain Scabbard was hurt, and Rusty was really enjoying himself. "Quite a guy, aren't you, Scabbard? How's it feel to be down on the ground looking up at a better man than you are?" He aimed a kick at Scabbard.

I said he *aimed* a kick. It never landed. Archie Cramer, coming by to visit his friend, was just in time. Captain Scabbard told me later he had never seen a man move so fast—it was like an elephant with wings. To Rusty the wings were two huge, iron fists that slammed into him like one massive sledgehammer. Even before Rusty hit the ground it was as though Archie had forgotten him. He turned to help his friend, Captain Scabbard.

Only after Archie had helped Captain Scabbard back to his chair and was sure he had not been seriously hurt did he again turn his attention to Rusty, who was still lying dazed where he had fallen. Archie picked him up as though he were a featherweight (actually he was a six footer weighing at least 185), carried him over to where Captain Scabbard was sitting, and forced him to his knees.

Rusty, coward that he was, was whimpering, "Captain, I meant no harm. I wouldn't have hurt you. Honest. Don't let him hit me again—please!" He looked up at Archie, but Archie, usually a friendly, good-natured man, was not inclined to listen to any pleas for mercy. The cowardly attack on his friend, who was helpless at the time, was too much for him, and it was only when Captain Scabbard spoke that his expression softened.

"Archie, let him go. I don't think he'll be back."

Archie loosened his grip, and Rusty was off like a scared rabbit.

Then there's Bob Culpepper. National pistol shooting champion (eight times). A real lawman. Whenever a tough case comes up in police circles they send for Detective Culpepper. Bob has been around a long time and has worked with Captain Scabbard on more than one occasion. He's a quiet man, not given to much talk, but Captain Scabbard has no truer friend.

Just one more. Talk about speed! Tony Cannon is short and slim, but many a long-legged speedster who thought he could outrun Tony learned the hard way that no one, and I mean *no one*, could move like this human gazelle. I won't give you his time on the hundred yard dash—you wouldn't believe it anyway. Tony Cannon is fast.

Scabbard's wife, Sally, knew how much her husband enjoyed the companionship of these men and had planned a get-together. It was mid-summer. Billy and Lisa, the two children, were away at camp, and Sally was happily willing to cook for the entire group for a long weekend— Friday, Saturday, and Sunday. So there they were, all of them, at the Scabbards' riverfront home, far out in the country, enjoying real home cooking.

"Sally, honey, this sure is good," Scabbard said.

Archie, speaking with his mouth full (one of his few bad habits, which his girlfriend was trying to correct), mumbled, "Terrific!"

Bob Culpepper chimed in. "I've never enjoyed food so much in my life. You know, Al, if I could be sure of getting as good a cook, I think I might be inclined to get married."

"Delectable—an exquisite epulation. Truly a culinary masterpiece," said Professor William Lemuel Perriwinkle, III.

Sally smiled happily. "Glad you like it; enjoy yourselves. If you need me, I'll be in the kitchen."

As Sally left the room, Captain Scabbard leaned forward, his smile fading and his voice low and serious. "Fellows, I believe God has brought us together this weekend for a purpose. Sally planned this months ago but—" He stopped and smiled as Sally entered with a fresh pot of coffee.

"Here's some more coffee, fellas. Hope I didn't interrupt anything."

"Thanks, honey," said Al, and Sally kissed

him and turned back to the kitchen. Al waited a moment, then continued. "What I need to discuss with you is top secret, so I can't even tell Sally. Just a week ago our friend Bill Perriwinkle received the first of three threatening notes. He refuses to take them seriously, but I do, and I think you all will when you see them. Bill didn't want me to bother you with them—thought it would interfere with our weekend together—but I know I speak for all of us when I say that if anyone is trying to get at Bill he will have to go through all of us." He looked around the table. Archie, sitting next to Perriwinkle, already had one of his huge hands on Bill's shoulder; Bob, on the other side, had his arm around Bill, and Tony got up and stood behind him.

"There you are, friend," said Captain Scabbard. "Did you think for a moment we'd let you try to handle this alone?"

Professor Perriwinkle, perhaps for the first time in his life, had no words ready. He knew words—long ones, short ones, and medium ones—but there was no way to describe how he felt just then. He had been more worried by the notes than he had cared to admit, even to himself, but now, with men like this surrounding him, he felt safe enough to face how frightened he was. When Bill had first received the notes, he had prayed that the Lord would somehow quiet his fears. God was now answering his prayer through Scabbard, Archie, Bob, and Tony, men who were Bill's brothers in Christ.

Captain Scabbard spread out the notes for all to see. Archie Cramer looked puzzled. "Notes? why these are just inventory lists. Just a lot of figures. Nothing to be scared of here, is there?"

Tony Cannon was about to agree when Captain Scabbard said, "That's what I thought too, Archie, but why would an 'inventory list' be clipped to Bill's morning newspaper on July twenty-second, twenty-sixth, and twenty-eighth? As you know, Bob Culpepper and I were visiting Bill on July twenty-second, the day the first list came. Bill wondered how it had gotten clipped to his newspaper and intended to throw it away, but then decided to show it to us. Bob thought it a bit strange and suggested we study it a bit. Actually it was Bill who finally figured it out. He noticed that the highest number was twenty-six, and assumed that somehow the alphabet was a key. From then on it was easy; that is, it was easy for the professor. I'll give you the key to the code later* but, for the moment, let's see what this 'inventory list' looks like. Bill has written out the decoded message on the right side of the paper."

*See end of story for code. Try to figure out how Bill broke the code to get the message before you look at the key.

```
part #      Bin # 1—2—3—4—5—6—7—8—9—10
26                 14—24—18
16                 15—3—22—18—19
10                 21—12—25
7                  23—18—1—7—25—19—22—11
23                 18—14—5
7                  22—18
```

MAKE
COPIES
JULY
26
WEAR
TIE

Archie and Tony studied the unusual code for a few minutes but could not make any sense of it.

Captain Scabbard explained. "Here's the story. You know the professor's reputation. When it comes to putting words together, there's none better. Our government knows this, and last month he was honored by a telephone call from the president of the United States. (Now what do you think of our friend?) The president requested Bill to help the State Department in a very important exchange of correspondence with one of the oil-producing countries.

"Bill can't tell us the name of the country, but our government is working out an agreement with their leaders, and it requires a lot of correspondence. Bill was asked to check those letters. He knows their language as well as he knows English. It's extremely important that there be no misunderstanding between the two governments, and it is Bill's job to make sure we understand exactly what the other country is saying, and that our letters to them are clear and to the point. It's a tough, important assignment, and I doubt if anyone but Bill could handle it.

"Now here's the problem. Someone who has no right to this information must have gotten wind of what's going on and is demanding copies of these top secret letters. We don't know who it is, whether an American traitor or a foreign spy, but these notes show that someone is determined to get this information. Look at these other notes. They too looked like 'inventory lists,' but Bill had no trouble deciphering them." Captain Scabbard laid two more papers on the table.

part #	Bin # 1—2—3—4—5—6—7—8—9—10
12	14—19—7
16	8—14—1—16—18
10	21—12—25
7	23—18—1—7—25—19—18—9—18—1

LAST CHANCE JULY 27

part #	Bin # 1—2—3—4—5—6—7—8—9—10
18	22—20—8—7
15	5
25	15—21—5—18
4	18—14—4

EIGHT OR YOU'RE DEAD

Bob Culpepper took over. "Even though Bill decoded the first note, it meant nothing to Al and me except that someone was demanding that Bill make copies of something or other by July 26. Knowing that Bill never wears a tie, they were demanding that he wear one to prove he was obeying orders. Bill was not at liberty to tell us anything until he had contacted the official in the State Department to whom he was directly responsible. Bill did so, also telling him that Captain Scabbard and I had seen the notes.

"It may give you some idea of the importance of Perriwinkle's work when I tell you that on that same day the secretary of state flew in to see him. Al and I had met the secretary some time ago when we were able to serve our government on a minor matter, and he gave permission for Bill to give us the whole story. We also told him of our coming get-together—Sally had already invited you fellows for this weekend—and asked him if our whole group could be of help. Although the secretary did not know either Tony or Archie, he did give us permission to let you know what was going on. It's up to you. Do you want to get involved or—?"

Archie and Tony looked at each other. Tony was the first to speak. "Bob, don't you see we *are* involved? Bill's our friend; he's in danger. What did you think we would say?" He looked again at Archie.

"Couldn't have said it better myself, Tony," said Archie.

Bob Culpepper smiled. "I was so sure of your answer that I have already volunteered for all of us. We are now working with Professor Perriwinkle in an official capacity. If things get too rough, I am authorized to call in the FBI. However, for the present, it was thought best to keep this quiet and see if we could find out who is back of these notes and block their plans. As of this moment we have full authority, in writing, to act as agents for the United States government."

Archie and Tony looked very solemn. They had never been in anything like that before. They wanted with all their hearts to help their friend, but—suppose they failed. Not only would Bill be in trouble, but their country would suffer. There was silence for a moment, then, "Captain," said Tony, "I'd feel much better if we prayed about this."

"Just what I was going to suggest, Tony," said Captain Scabbard. "I said earlier that God brought us together for a purpose. Let's place ourselves in His hands and ask for His help." All five men went to their knees and prayed that God would be with them. None of them prayed for their personal safety, only that they would be worthy of their Lord.

As they rose, Captain Scabbard took the lead. "Today is July twenty-eighth, the date mentioned in note number three—'Eight or you're dead.'

Perriwinkle is almost always home by ten o'clock, and I suggest that tonight be no exception. Let's not do anything to let our 'inventory' boys know that anyone but Bill has read their coded notes. Bill's bike is outside. It's half past eight. He'll just have time to reach home by ten. Here's what we'll do.

At twenty minutes before ten, two men stood in the shadows near the professor's home. "This is the place, Freddy," said one of them, a huge, dark-haired fellow. "The boss told us that the one we're after should be riding up on a bike about ten. I don't know what he looks like, but he'll be no trouble. He's a college prof. You know what to do."

Freddy nodded. "Yeah, Bull, we're just supposed to rough him up a bit, throw a scare into him, then beat it. Right?"

Bull pulled Freddy back into the shadows. "Look, stupid, you're standing right out in the open. What if the prof sees us and keeps peddling? I'll be glad when this is over. Man, could I stand a drink. Y'know, I've been on the wagon for two days. Hey, I almost forgot. Here, take these cutters and nip that telephone wire over there. We don't want anyone phoning the police."

The two men stood silently for about ten minutes, then Bull grabbed Freddy's arm. "Here comes a bike. Must be the prof. Looks bigger than what the boss said, but it must be him—get a load of those big glasses. Wait till he gets off the bike and starts walkin'. *Now!*"

The bike rider had reached Perriwinkle's house. As he dismounted and started up the front walk, Bull and Freddy closed in. Bull made a grab for the big glasses perched on the bike rider's nose while Freddy reached out to pin down his arms. Bull had just started to say something like, "Sorry, buddy, just carryin' out orders," when he found himself sitting on the ground holding what later proved to be a broken nose. Freddy was next as the "prof" ducked a wild left and planted a solid smash on Freddy's jaw. Both men went down, got up, and then went down again as the bike rider burst into action. Bull, down for the third time, yelled to Freddy, "Let's get out of here fast; I've had it with this 'prof.' Wait till I see the boss."

Both men started off. Captain Scabbard picked up his glasses and calmly continued on his way into Professor Perriwinkle's house. Bull and Freddy had just about reached the sidewalk when they ran into Archie, who had driven up in Captain Scabbard's car with Bob Culpepper, Tony Cannon, and Bill Perriwinkle. Archie reached out and collared both men, holding them as easily as though they were two Perriwinkles. "Well, well,

82

what have we here? You fellows look as though you were leaving the scene of an accident. That's against the law, you know. Let's go into the house and talk this over.''

Bull and Freddy attempted some resistance, but Archie just smiled and dragged them along. Once Bull fired a kick at Archie's ankle, but before it landed his neck was almost broken as Archie effortlessly tightened his grip.

What a day it had been for Bull and Freddy. An easy job, roughing up a little college professor, had turned into a nightmare. Their orders had been to ''mess him up a bit, throw a scare into him, then beat it.'' But instead of the professor, the two amateur crooks first met Captain Scabbard, then Archie—like going from a tiger to an elephant. Nothing was said until, as they were entering the professor's house, Bull noticed Bill Perriwinkle for the first time. ''Hey, you must be the guy we were supposed to work over. You look like a real easy mark—but that hunk of lightning on the bike! Freddy, we were tricked.'' Freddy said nothing. His jaw hurt too badly.

As they entered the house, Captain Scabbard said, ''Archie, let's get these men into the basement and have a talk with them. Bill, can we cover the basement windows so that no one outside will know we're here? I rather think you'll have visitors, and it would be best if they thought you were alone.''

Perriwinkle thought for a moment. "Yes, Al, you can use part of the basement that has been made into a room. There's only one window, and I can easily cover that so no light will show."

Soon they were all in the professor's basement, and, after the window was darkened, Captain Scabbard questioned Bull. "You may as well tell us the whole story now. If not, the police will get it out of you, and they may not be as easy on you as Archie and I have been." Bull growled something about "if that was bein' easy, I'd hate to run into you when you was tough," then, "OK, what do you want to know?"

"First, the men who sent you. Who are they, and why did they want Professor Perriwinkle beaten up?"

"Look, mister," said Bull, "all I know is two guys came up to us in a bar and asked us if we wanted to earn some easy money. They said they wanted to teach a lesson to some professor who had tried to make a fool of them. I don't know who they was. All they told us about the professor was where he lived and that he would be ridin' up on his bike about ten o'clock. They didn't say nothin' about professor's friends. If we knew what was comin', we wouldn't have taken the job for no kind of money."

"What did they tell you to do after you have beaten up the professor?" asked Detective Culpepper.

"Do? They didn't tell us to do nothin'; just make sure the prof ain't too bad hurt to get up and then beat it away as fast as we could. They said they'd take over from there. Said they'd meet us later at the bar and pay off. Now I guess we ain't gonna get nothin'. What a mess."

Then, looking at Captain Scabbard, he said, "Hey, didn't I hear someone call you Scabbard? You must be *Captain* Scabbard. Man, if I knew you was mixed up in this I wouldn't have touched it with a ten-foot pole. What the boys say about you is true; I don't want to meet you again— never!"

Captain Scabbard smiled. "I'm sorry, Bull, about the beating I gave you, but after all, two men your size ganging up on a friend of mine was a bit too much. We'll talk about that later. Perhaps you may yet be glad you met me. I do have some good news I hope to share with you later. Right now we have work to do. I'm sorry, but we'll have to gag you and your friend. Any sound from you could ruin the plan I have in mind. Archie, you and Tony take care of this, will you? Bob, let's go upstairs and help Bill get ready for a visit." Then, with a glance at Archie, he added, "I don't think Bull or Freddy will give you any more trouble. They know by now, I'm sure, that we mean business." Bull said nothing, but Freddy spoke for both of them. "Look, Captain Scabbard, we had enough. You won't get a peep out of us. Just make that big moose promise to keep his fists quiet."

Captain Scabbard, Bob Culpepper, and Bill Perriwinkle went upstairs to the professor's study, a spacious, cheerful room with three large windows facing the street. "Here's what I have in mind," said Captain Scabbard. "We'll put some bandages on Bill's face and around his head, to make it appear he's been pretty badly hurt. Then he'll sit at his desk as though he's working on some papers. The men we're expecting will think everything has gone according to plan. Bob and I will conceal ourselves in the next room."

Bob Culpepper spoke up. "Al, I suggest we set up a tape recorder. It may come in handy as evidence."

"Good idea, Bob," said Al. "We can take this one from Bill's desk and hide it, OK?"

"Just one thought," said Bob. "I see Bill has a remote switch. It will take only a moment to connect it up, then we can control it from the next room."

While Bob Culpepper was wiring the switch, Captain Scabbard went outside and moved his car to the shadows behind Perriwinkle's home. When he returned, the two men worked on Professor Perriwinkle's face so that it appeared that Bull and Freddy had carried out their assignment. Everything was now in order. Bill sat working at his desk; Captain Scabbard and Bob Culpepper were in the next room. Archie and Tony were told of the plan and waited quietly in the basement until they were needed. Eleven fifteen—nothing to do but wait. Captain Al Scabbard and his friends were ready.

A few minutes after midnight, a long, black sedan with dimmed headlights came slowly up the street, coming almost to a stop as it passed Professor Perriwinkle's house. Moving about a hundred yards beyond his house, it turned and came back, again slowing almost to a stop. Professor Perriwinkle, well bandaged, sat in full view, working busily at his desk. The car stopped and three men got out, walked to the front door, and knocked. Professor Perriwinkle limped slowly to the door and, without opening it, called out, "What is it you want?"

"I think you know," said one of the men. "You're lucky to be alive. Now you know we mean business, so let's get this over with."

Bill opened the door slowly, playing his part well. "Haven't you done enough? Can't you just let me alone? You know I can't give you copies of the letters you're after. The government checks my every move, and they would be sure to find out. Then what good would the copies do you?"

"Look, friend, we want copies—*now!* Bull and Freddy gave you a taste of what happens to anyone holding out on us. Just a taste. It's up to you. Are you going to be reasonable, or do we do it the hard way—hard for you, that is?"

Professor Perriwinkle, as though almost afraid to open his mouth, asked what possible use they could have for the letters. One of them laughed and said, "Well, it's really none of your business, but we have a deal, and the letters are worth a cool million to our customer. Now let's cut out the talk. Time's up, prof."

With this, he and his two companions surrounded Perriwinkle. One of them pinned his arms behind his back, another took out a short length of rope, and the third sat behind his back in the desk chair directing the proceedings. "I said time's up and I meant it. Did you ever feel a rope around your neck, pulling tighter and tighter while you're fighting for breath? It's not pleasant. Get started, Joe. Let's see how much our educated friend can take."

Professor Perriwinkle was helpless as Joe moved into position and slipped the rope around his neck, then waited for instructions.

"All right, Joe, take it nice and easy." To Perriwinkle he said, "We want copies of *all* the letters, all of them. We know they're here somewhere. Joe's going to start pulling. All you have to do is tell us where the letters are and everything will be fine. Hold out on us and—" He sat back with his feet on the desk. Joe started on his deadly chore, gently pulling the rope tighter and tighter.

Up to that point Captain Scabbard and Bob Culpepper had waited quietly as each word was being recorded. They were sure that the men were bluffing and that no real harm would come to Professor Perriwinkle. But now—Bob Culpepper with his hand on Al Scabbard's shoulder could feel the captain's body stiffen as he watched his friend beginning to gasp for breath. Bluff or no bluff, Captain Scabbard had reached his limit. He burst savagely from his place of concealment. Captain Scabbard was *mad*.

His first target was Joe. Joe never saw what hit him as he crumpled to the floor, the rope falling from his hands. The other two men jumped Scabbard, trying to down him by sheer weight. Two against one. Scabbard sidestepped, then was on them like a tornado. All the years of trying to control his fierce temper seemed to mean nothing. What those men were doing to his friend Perriwinkle, first in sending Bull and Freddy, and now in the cowardly attempt to make him talk, was more than he could stomach. Instead of helping Scabbard as he intended to do, Bob Culpepper found himself trying to prevent Al from literally tearing the men to pieces. Archie erupted from the basement and joined Bob in holding back Captain Scabbard, but not before all three bullies were sprawled unconscious on the floor.

Captain Scabbard regained control of himself quickly. No one knew better than he the importance of self-control, and he made no excuse for losing his temper. He quickly confessed it to his Lord and prayed for forgiveness. Then he planned the next move.

As he spoke quietly with his friends, Captain Scabbard noticed that two of the prone men were regaining consciousness. One of them, not knowing that he was being observed, nudged the other and pointed to a clock hanging on the study wall. That had to mean something, but what? There was no use asking the men; they would pretend ignorance, and yet—there was something. Captain Scabbard thought for a moment, then said, "Tie these men up. We'll notify the FBI. We've done all we can do."

After the men were tied up, Captain Scabbard motioned his friends into an adjoining room, then told them what he had seen. Professor Perriwinkle came up with an idea. "The recorder—is it still operational? Most auspicious. Let them alone for a few minutes; they're bound to talk. Notice their proximity to the recorder; every syllable will be clearly taped. Listen, aren't they conversing now?" A low murmur came from Bill's study, and although no words could be distinguished, it was evident that the professor was right as usual.

Ten minutes went by. Nothing further was heard, and Archie and the captain went to Bill's study and carried the prisoners into another room. Then Bob Culpepper set up the recorder for playback. First they heard the men knock on the door, Bill's timid answer, and the threat of what was going to happen if the letter copies were not handed over immediately. They could hear Perriwinkle gasping for breath as the rope was tightened about his neck. Suddenly the tape thundered with what seemed like an explosion, then a series of thuds as Captain Scabbard took charge. For a time there was silence. It was necessary to turn the volume up, but still they could hear quite clearly.

"Carl, you knew what I meant when I pointed to the clock, didn't you? Well, anyway, we don't have a thing to worry about. We can forget about Scabbard calling the FBI. I checked when we got here, and Bull had already cut the telephone wires. Before we left, I had a call from the Baron himself, and he instructed Johnnie to bring ten of his men here by one o'clock. If everything's OK, I'm to meet them at the road. If I'm *not* there, Johnnies going to surround the house and take over." He paused. "Scabbard's in for a surprise. He won't have a chance. Johnnie has two bullet-proof cars, machine guns, tear gas—you name it. Just about fifteen minutes to go. All we have to do is keep Scabbard and his boys talking until Johnnie gets here." The voice again paused, then chuckled. "Good thing we noticed that car out back." The other man laughed.

"Nobody's going to drive *that* hack until they get a new set of tires—that was some job you did with that ice pick!"

Here the voices stopped, and Bob Culpepper reached over and switched off the recorder. Captain Scabbard looked at his watch. About ten minutes to go, no telephone, and no car. Now what? There was only one answer: Tony Cannon, the human greyhound. Al called him from the basement where he was standing guard over Bull and Freddy.

"Tony, I don't know whether you can make it in time, but it's our only chance. Somehow we must contact Lieutenant Grainger of the state police. The nearest house is about a mile east of here, but there's always a question whether anyone would open up to someone knocking at their door at this hour. Remember that gas station we passed on the way here this evening? I would guess that's a couple of miles. Greg Fillmore, who owns it, lives in the house across the road. He's used to being called on at all hours for emergency service. Tell him I sent you. He often has contact with Lieutenant Grainger on towing wrecked cars, so I'm sure he'll be able to get hold of him in short order."

Captain Scabbard gave Tony a quick summary of the recorded conversation with a warning. "This fellow Johnnie must be almost here. If you see headlights, head for the high grass on the side of the road. We'll be praying for you."

Tony Cannon was off and running. A better word might be flying. Those slender legs of his were a blur of action, his feet barely touching the ground. Then a sudden glare of headlights as a heavy car, with another immediately following, rounded a turn in the road. Tony dived for cover and lay motionless. Had he been seen?

The lead car skidded to a halt so quickly that the other car narrowly averted a collision. "Any of you guys see anything? Switch on your spotlight—over here. Now up and down the road, slow and easy."

Tony lay motionless, hardly breathing, remembering Captain Scabbard's words. "We'll be praying for you." The light danced over him, passed on, then back and forth over the heavy growth in which he lay.

"Probably just an animal, Johnnie. Maybe a deer. There's lots of them in this part of the country."

Johnnie seemed satisfied. "OK, let's move on. We must be almost there." He muttered something that Tony could not make out and drove off.

Tony, after waiting until both cars were almost

94

out of sight, was off again. Just as he reached the road, a voice rang out. "Hold it, buster, or you're a dead man." Johnnie, not quite satisfied, had left one of his men behind, and Tony had fallen into the trap. Keeping to the edge of the road, Tony rocketed from side to side, bent forward almost double. He felt a sharp stab of pain in his left arm as a bullet from the gunman found its mark. Two more whined by him harmlessly. Tony was not beyond firing range but kept on at blinding speed until there was no longer any chance of pursuit. Now he checked his arm and was encouraged to find it was only a minor flesh wound with very little bleeding.

Breathing a prayer of thanks, he continued until he saw, in the distance, in huge letters, Greg Fillmore—Gas. Across the road, as Captain Scabbard had said, was a frame house. Tony made his way to the house and was soon pounding at the door. "Hey, young fella, cut it out. I can hear ya." Tony looked up. This must be Greg Fillmore, a big, good-natured man grinning at him although it was evident he had just awakened. "Mr. Fillmore, Captain Scabbard sent me. He needs help. Can you get hold of the state police? Please hurry."

"Well, I'll be—I'm on my way, young fella. Now," he said as he appeared at the door, "you sit and catch your breath a minute. I'll get

Lieutenant Grainger on the phone, and you can talk directly to him."

After Tony had left, Captain Scabbard, Bob Culpepper, and the professor went back to the room with Carl and his two companions. Archie went down to the basement to check on Bull and Freddy, who were still tied and gagged. The professor switched out all the lights, leaving the house in complete darkness.

Carl was the first to speak. "I know you guys. You're Captain Scabbard." To Culpepper he said, "Didn't I run into you a couple of years ago? Sure, you're a detective, aren't you? Look, we have nothing against you; all we're after is a few letters. Why don't you fellows just mind your own business? You might as well know you can't stop us. Nobody can stop us. Let us go, no one will get hurt, and each of you including the professor, will get one thousand dollars."

Captain Scabbard just smiled. He knew Carl was stalling for time. "Carl," he said quietly, "you may as well know that your two friends, Bull and Freddy, are resting in the basement. They ran into a little trouble before they could carry out their plans. Now you three fellows haven't done much better. What makes you think things will be different from now on?"

Carl sneered. "You're pretty sure of yourselves, aren't you? The great Captain Scabbard, Culpepper, the world's number one detective, and the brilliant Professor Perriwinkle. None of you stand a chance with the man I'm really working for. Someday you'll meet him, but it will be too late. Give up now and he'll go easy on you—try to fight him and you're a goner."

"It's interesting," said Captain Scabbard, "that you should talk about this superman you claim to be working for. Tell me more about him. He must be quite a man."

Carl's two companions glared at him and he pressed his lips together, determined to say no more. Captain Scabbard could see that he was badly frightened and had already said too much about whoever it was that really controlled him and his gang.

There was silence for a few moments, then Captain Scabbard said, "It's only fair to tell you that we are working directly under the United States government. You men are prisoners of the FBI. If you think your leader can get you out of this, you must have a lot of faith in him. Speaking of leaders, my friends and I have a Leader far above your man or even the president of the United States. A Leader against whom no man can stand. Someday you must meet Him. You can meet Him *now* as your Savior or—"

"I've heard that religious stuff before," interrupted Carl. "I'll take my chances. All I want now is to make as much money as I can, no matter how. My man pays off in cash."

As he spoke there was a sound of cars outside and then a voice. "Carl—Carl—are you there?—Answer me."

"Hear that?" said Carl. "That's our boys out there, ten of them with machine guns. What's your God going to do now? Why don't you pray or whatever you do when you need help? See how much good it will do you."

"We have already prayed," said Captain Scabbard, smiling. "You may not believe it, but the answer came even before we had finished." He pulled his small Testament from his pocket and quoted 1 Peter 3:13: " 'Who is he that will harm you, if ye be followers of that which is good?' Those are the words of my Leader. That's enough for me."

Again the voice from outside called, "Carl, this is Johnnie. Answer me."

Carl opened his mouth as if to answer, but it was Joe who suddenly yelled, "Johnnie, this is Joe! They've got us, but you can handle them. No guns, just a few Bible-reading guys having a prayer meeting. Get us out of this, and you'll be a big man with the Baron."

"You fool!" screamed Carl, turning deathly white. "You stupid fool. You'll get us all killed."

Calling to Johnnie, he said, "Forget what Joe said. Just get us out of here. We'll deal with Joe later."

Everything was quiet for almost five minutes. Then everyone in the house heard the sound of cars being started. Captain Scabbard went to the window and could hardly believe his eyes. Johnnie and his men were jumping into the two cars they had brought as though in panic. Moments later they were careening down the road at top speed. Why? Was this a trap of some sort? Bob Culpepper and Perriwinkle joined Al at the window.

"Fellows, I don't know what to make of this," said Captain Scabbard. "For the moment I think we had better just stay as we are. Perhaps they got a message over their radio, perhaps—" Then softly so that the three prisoners could not hear, "Did you notice Carl's reaction when Joe mentioned the name 'Baron'? Even in the darkness I could tell that he was scared stiff. I've heard rumors of the Baron, but never connected him with this affair. I wonder—"

Culpepper was about to answer when Bill excitedly pointed to a faint glow in the distance. Could it be Johnnie and his men returning? As the glow brightened, they could make out headlights of at least five cars, then the sound of sirens. Tony had done his job. In a well-planned move, the five police cars surrounded the house, ready for action.

Captain Scabbard told the professor to switch on the lights, then called out, "Lieutenant

Grainger, this is Captain Scabbard. Everything is under control. I'm coming out." He opened the door and, as he walked toward the nearest car, he saw Tony Cannon jump out. He was immediately pulled back.

"Hold it, young fella. Let's be sure this is all on the up and up. Perhaps someone has a gun on the captain. I'll handle this my way." Then in a loud voice he said, "I'm coming in. All my men are armed with machine guns. Any false moves and we'll pepper this place full of holes." As he spoke, he advanced toward Captain Scabbard, gun drawn, ready for action.

"Thank you, Lieutenant," said Captain Scabbard. "I should have known you wouldn't take any chances. I can assure you there's no funny business going on. Come in and I'll give you the whole story."

That about wrapped it up for the gang that had tried to scare Professor Perriwinkle into surrendering copies of the confidential letters he was translating—at least for five members of the gang. Carl, Joe, Bull, and the others were handcuffed by Lieutenant Grainger's men and hustled off to prison. Later they would be tried in a federal court and found guilty. Professor Perriwinkle continued on with his work, and in a few weeks a satisfactory agreement was worked out between the United States Government and the oil-producing country. Perhaps someday we can give full details, but for the present the entire matter is classified information.

It was several months later that Professor Perriwinkle, pedaling his bike with every bit of strength he possessed, sailed into Captain Scabbard's driveway, jumped off, letting the bike crash into the garage, and pounded furiously on the door. Captain Scabbard was intently reading a letter when he heard this terrific banging. Sally was on her way to the door, but Al took over. Someone banging away like that might be dangerous.

"Bill Perriwinkle, what in the world?" The professor, looking somewhat sheepish, smiled at Sally and Captain Scabbard. "I'm sorry, I guess I am a bit overexcited." He was speaking so quickly that he forgot to use big words. "But I wanted you to be the first to see this letter. After all, it's you and my other friends that deserve the credit. You know, of course, that after all the trouble we had, I continued on with my work. I did my best but, you know how it is, in something as important as this there is always the fear that it wasn't good enough. Today I received this letter, a *personal* letter from the *president himself!* Handwritten, too. Al, I didn't fully realize the pressure I was under until this letter came and I knew all was well."

Bill Perriwinkle calmed down a bit and became the professor. After all, the use of one and two syllable words was not worthy of Professor Perriwinkle. "Captain Scabbard, I am rendered inarticulate; for the first time in my life I am verbally barren."

"Come on in and have a seat, Bill," said Sally, laughing. "I've never seen you so excited. We both want to read the letter."

"Tell you what we should do, Bill," said Captain Scabbard when they were comfortably seated. "Let's call Bob, Archie, and Tony. It's about five o'clock now, and I think they'll all be home by six. We can call them then and share the good news. I'm sure they're going to be as excited as you. Perhaps not verbally barren or inarticulate, but excited."

Bill grinned; he was used to Scabbard's good-natured kidding. "Good idea. Mind if I stick around for an hour?"

"As a matter of fact, Bill, I was going to get in touch with you anyway. I too have a letter, and, though not as pleasant as yours, it is interesting. Notice the envelope: no return address, postmarked New York City, where any possibility of tracing it is out of the question. Here, read it for yourself."

To Captain Scabbard

Respected Sir:

You won a battle—not the war. I underestimated you. Actually I did not know you were such a close friend of Professor Perriwinkle or my course of action would have been far more sophisticated. I have lost five men, a mere nothing. The letters—they were more important, but there are always fresh opportunities.

May I advise you to not get in my way again. I have resources you little dream of. You were fortunate once. Be thankful. If there is a next time, I'll crush you.

You may wonder why Johnnie and my men drove off that night. I'll tell you so that you will know that every move my men make is planned to the last detail. When your Tony Cannon reached Police Lt. Grainger, I knew exactly what was going on. Very little happens without my knowledge. As always my men were equipped with the latest in communication devices and I radioed Johnnie to leave immediately rather than confront a superior force.

Farewell, Captain Scabbard. Don't let success go to your head. Your book says that pride goes before a fall. Your time is limited

The Baron

All the bounce seemed to go out of Professor Perriwinkle. "What are you going to do, Al? What chance do you or any of us have against this, this—?"

"Do? Bill, I don't intend to do anything." Captain Scabbard answered firmly. "Perhaps the Baron and I will meet again. It's not my choice to make. I have already followed the example of Hezekiah and shared this with the Lord.* When he received a threatening letter, he spread it out before God. I have done the same. God never changes. I can trust Him just as Hezekiah did. Whatever happens between the Baron and me is for the Lord to decide."

Bill visibly relaxed, then smiled. "Al, with all my study, my greatest need is to know the Lord as you do."

Key to Code
Step 1: Write out the alphabet *A* through *M* on one line, then *N* through *Z* on a second line below the first.

*Isaiah 37:14.

Step 2: Start at N, number it 1, then draw a solid line first to B, then P, then D, and so on to Z. Number each letter consecutively, with Z becoming 13. Then draw a broken line from A to O, then to C, and so on to M, continuing to number each letter. Note that all top-line letters are even numbers, all lower-line letters are odd numbers.

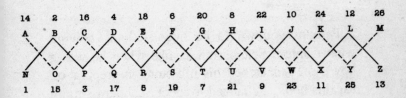

The first message to Bill:

Part #   Bin # 1—2—3—4—5—6—7—8—9—10

26   14—24—18
M   A K E

16   15—3—22—18—19
C   O P I E S

and so on.

105

4

A Case of Character

Perhaps you would be interested in knowing what Captain Scabbard was like when he was a boy. As I researched his life story in preparation for this book, I chanced to meet Scabbard's ninth grade football coach, a Mr. Mack Taylor. When I acquainted him with my interest in Al Scabbard, he beamed. For more than two hours, he talked nonstop about his recollections of Captain Scabbard. One particular story that Coach Taylor related will give you, I think, a pretty good idea how a boy develops into a man like Captain Al Scabbard.

Al was fourteen years old. It was summertime, and Al was enjoying the vacation break between the eighth and ninth grades. One Thursday evening in July, as the family gathered for dinner, Al's dad announced, "An excellent job opportunity has just come up in Marketville. I've been praying about it for a few days now, and I sense the Lord may want us to move. The company must know my decision within two days. I want to discuss it with you and pray together as a family for God's clear guidance."

Al's younger sister Claudine loved anything different. Without any hesitation she happily said, "Sounds great to me. Can I have pink carpeting in my new bedroom?"

Al frowned, looked at his dinner plate for almost a minute, then looked up anxiously. "Dad, this next year I have a chance to be the regular first string quarterback at Newbury Junior High. They have a super team, and we have a great chance to win the regional championship again, maybe even the state."

Al's dad looked understandingly at his upset son. He knew that during his previous school year Al had started in half the games for the Junior High varsity squad and had displayed great potential to be a star. At the end of last year's football season, Newbury's coach had written a letter to Mr. Scabbard, expressing his confidence that Al could next year lead the team to an undefeated season.

When Mr. Scabbard had learned of the job offer in Marketville, he immediately checked into the local junior high school's athletic program. He discovered that Hamilton Consolidated, Marketville's junior and senior high school, had begun football competition only two years earlier, and in their first two seasons had not won a single game. Mr. Scabbard recalled a preseason practice game during the previous year in which Al had easily quarterbacked Newbury past Hamilton by the landslide margin of thirty-four to nothing. The local newspaper had stated that the game was no test of Newbury's strength. Hamilton's biggest tackle weighed in at 128 pounds, their best receiver boasted a record of only two caught passes in ten contests, and their kicker was averaging punts of just under seventeen yards.

"Dad," Al started again, "if we do move, couldn't I stay here in Newbury and live with Aunt Marge and Uncle Dave? If I live in Marketville, I'd have to attend Hamilton Consolidated, and their football team is the laughingstock of the conference. They haven't won a game since they started playing. Dad," Al's voice choked, "I don't want to play for a bunch of losers."

Mr. Scabbard looked straight into his son's moist eyes. "Al, I can appreciate your feelings. I'd rather play for Newbury, too, if I were your age. Let's commit the decision to the Lord. And Al," Mr. Scabbard's voice softened, "I hope you'll be open to whatever the Lord has for us."

Al nodded glumly, then picked at his dinner without saying a word to anyone. He spent the rest of the evening in his bedroom with the door shut, lying flat on his back staring vacantly at the ceiling.

Two days later, as the Scabbard family sat down for supper, Al felt a tight knot in the middle of his stomach. He had heard his mother tell Claudine that tonight the decision would be made.

Mrs. Scabbard served up the meat loaf, french fries, and peas before Mr. Scabbard said a word. When everyone's plate was steaming with food, Mr. Scabbard cleared his throat and said, "Kids, your mother and I spent most of last night and a good part of today praying and discussing the decision. I believe that God wants us all to move to Marketville. Al, I wrestled with the thought of your staying here with Uncle Dave, but I think that for some reason the Lord wants all of us to move. Tomorrow our house will go on the market. We plan to move in a month."

Al stared at his dad in unbelief. "But Dad," Al objected, "I don't understand why—" and then he stopped. Long ago he had learned that complaining and arguing with his dad never got him what he wanted.

Within two weeks, their house sold. Al overheard his dad comment to his mother that the Lord seemed to be blessing their decision to move by selling the house so quickly. Right on schedule, one month from the day they decided to move, the Scabbard family watched their furniture fill the small van that would move them from Newbury to Marketville.

Marketville was a pleasant little country town, with rows of stately old trees shading the streets in the residential area. Downtown Marketville boasted one movie theater, which consistently played last season's hits, two drug stores, a new professional office building, a large modern department store, and a few dozen shops, stores, and restaurants. Hamilton Junior-Senior High was located one mile west of town on a lazy, sprawling campus complete with a life-size statue of Wilbur Hamilton, the town's first mayor, in front of the main entrance.

On September 6, Al Scabbard walked for the first time past Wilbur's marble frown through the front door of Hamilton High. As Al entered the small lobby, he quickly noticed the words Football Tryouts displayed in large letters on the school's bulletin board. With halfhearted interest, he shuffled over to the board and read the handwritten announcement.

All 8th and 9th GRADE BOYS WHO WANT TO TRY OUT FOR THE HAMILTON JUNIOR HIGH FOOTBALL TEAM, REPORT TO THE ATHLETIC FIELD AT 3:30 PROMPT THURSDAY AFTERNOON, SEPTEMBER 9. COME IN GYM CLOTHES AND SNEAKERS.

An eighth grade boy walked up next to Al, read the announcement out loud with obvious excitement, then turned to Al and nearly shouted, "Hey, football practice this Thursday! Man, I can hardly wait!"

Al looked straight ahead and snapped, "A decent team would have started practice weeks ago in summer camp. Newbury High even has spring training. But then this is Hamilton." Al turned and walked away, leaving the enthusiastic eighth grader with his head tilted to one side, looking puzzled and a bit disheartened.

Thursday afternoon soon arrived. A few minutes past three found over fifty junior high boys behind the school, milling around uncertainly on the large open grassy area that served as the athletic field. During the winter months, a few changes converted the area into a soccer field, and when spring arrived, a crew of volunteer students did their best with rakes and chalk lines to reclaim it as a baseball diamond.

At 3:30 sharp, a short, broad-shouldered, husky man, not quite old enough to be called middle-aged, jogged onto the field and blew his whistle.

"There's Coach Taylor," Al overheard one would-be football player say to another. "Man, is he tough."

"OK, men," the coach bellowed. "Let's get

your names, then we'll see who around here wants to play football."

Three crooked lines were formed, one in front of Coach Taylor and the other two in front of volunteer assistant coaches. Most of the boys worked off their tension with lots of chatter and a few faked tackles. Al stood silently at the end of Coach Taylor's line, watching the proceedings with half-open eyes.

The lines moved slowly. After what seemed an hour, Taylor's whistle gathered fifty-one boys around him. "Two laps for starters—get moving," he barked.

Al strolled casually over to the poorly marked running area, made his legs begin a slow jog, then, halfway around the first lap, burst into a sprint that left fifty panting boys trailing far behind. When he finished the two laps, Coach Taylor greeted him with, "You run pretty fast. Maybe you can help the team." Al nodded without saying a word.

The first two weeks of practice established Al Scabbard as the most accurate, longest passer, and the shiftiest, best broken-field runner of all the boys. Clark Dentworth, the ninth grader who last year played second string quarterback, watched glumly as the Newbury High transplant guaranteed him another year on the bench. Al was good.

Word spread quickly that Al Scabbard, last

113

year's star for Newbury, was now wearing the red and blue of Hamilton High. The high school too, whose varsity team had every reason to expect another winless season, was buzzing with excitement. In a few short weeks, Al Scabbard had become a hero in the hallways of Hamilton High.

Two weeks later, on October 7, the Hamilton Hustlers (Coach Taylor had chosen the team name) played their first game at home. It was a clear, crisp Saturday afternoon. By game time, the stands were overflowing with excited Hamilton High students and supporters, all eagerly waiting to watch their new star lead the Hustlers to victory. The Whitemarsh Lions ran onto the field first. Two minutes later, when the red and blue Hustlers made their entrance, the stands went wild: pennants waving, horns tooting, and a loud chant, "We want Al, we want Al."

Mr. Scabbard, Al's father, was sitting high up in the bleachers, leaning back against the railing behind him, his hands folded in his lap. The only evidence that he was not perfectly relaxed was the almost noiseless steady tapping of his left foot on the floorboards beneath him.

The Hustlers won the toss and elected to receive. Derek Adams fumbled the kickoff at the 30-yard line, tried to pick it up, but instead kicked it backwards, and finally fell on the ball at the Hamilton 6-yard line.

On the first play from scrimmage, Al, starting at quarterback, threw a perfect bullet into the outstretched arms of Gary Brent, a wide-open receiver. The ball darted through his hands and bounced off his chest for an incomplete pass. On second down Al ran to his left and danced his way past five tacklers for a gain of fourteen yards. First down, Hamilton. Brent caught Al's next throw, for a gain of five yards, ran for two more, then fumbled. The Lions recovered on the Hustlers' 27-yard line. Three plays later, Mort Little, the Lions' tough fullback, bulled his way through Hamilton's weak defense for the first score of the game. Lions 6, Hamilton 0.

Four quarters later, Al Scabbard had collected a game high of forty-seven yards running, scored the Hustlers' only touchdown, and thrown sixteen perfect passes, only two of which were caught. Final score: Lions 37, Hustlers 6.

The fans who before were shouting madly filed quietly to their cars as the Hustlers slowly walked to their locker room. Al showered and quickly dressed without saying a word to any of his teammates. When he reached his dad's car, he climbed in, looked straight ahead, and said, "They're a bunch of turkeys." Al's dad said nothing.

The first half of the next game, played on the home field of the Malvern Maulers, was a repeat of the season's opener the week before. Al played brilliantly, the rest of the Hustlers made every mistake possible, and the Maulers stampeded through Hamilton's defense like a herd of elephants through a field of terrified goats.

During the halftime break, Coach Taylor shouted encouragement to his beaten dejected troops.

"Listen, men, the mark of greatness is to never quit. This team will improve. We have the talent to play well. If you lay down and play dead, then you aren't the men I think you are. Give it all you've got, and, win or lose, you'll have my respect."

Al sat in a corner bench by himself, dangling his helmet from his left arm, looking down at nothing in particular.

The Hustlers received the kickoff to open the second half. On the first play from scrimmage, Al took the snap from center and leisurely strolled backward as if he were politely getting out of someone's way. Just before the Mauler's lineman reached him, he threw the ball weakly, end over end, about ten yards into the eager arms of a green-shirted opponent. The surprised Mauler clutched the ball and scampered forty yards for a touchdown.

When the Hustlers regained possession of the ball, Al again took the first snap, then halfheartedly ran straight ahead. No gain. On the next play, he fumbled the ball; the Malvern Maulers recovered.

It was plain to everyone in the stands that the Hustlers' talented quarterback simply was not trying. The Mauler supporters joined the large group of Hustler fans who had traveled to see the game in a noisy chorus of boos. Coach Taylor paced in front of his bench, then stopped in front of Clark Dentworth.

"Dentworth, you're taking over at quarterback. Send Scabbard to the bench."

Al jogged lazily off the field, sat down, and watched his replacement assume command of the team. Dentworth labored valiantly, but he simply did not have the skill to do the job well. When the buzzer sounded ending the third quarter, the score was Hamilton 12 (both touchdowns scored by Al in the first half), Malvern 34.

Coach Taylor walked over to Al and asked, "Scabbard, do you want to play ball or not?"

Without raising his head, Al said, "Why bother? We haven't got a team."

The coach's face turned an angry red. "Scabbard," he ordered, "you're suspended. Take a shower, turn in your uniform, and don't report for practice till further notice. *Move*!"

Mr. Scabbard, again perched on the highest spot in the stands, watched everything. When Al left the bench and walked off in the direction of the locker room, he knew what had happened. He made his way down from the grandstand, went to the car, and waited.

He did not have to wait very long. Within fifteen minutes, Al found his way to the car and sat in the front seat next to his dad. Al slammed the door and repeated, "What a bunch of turkeys."

Mr. Scabbard turned toward his son, put his hand firmly on Al's shoulder, and slowly said, "Al, they may not have your talent, but they try. For the first time in my life, I am not proud to be your father."

The long drive home was in absolute silence.

The next few days around the Scabbard house were strained and uncomfortable. Al said very little. He came home from school as soon as classes were dismissed, laced up his sneakers to shoot a few baskets, came in to eat supper, then spent the evening in his room. The fifth night after the game, Al emerged from his room to get a snack. As he reached for an unopened jar of peanuts, he could overhear his mother talking to his dad in the living room.

"Honey, I'm so worried about Al. Shouldn't you speak to him?"

"I would do anything to help that boy," Al heard his dad say intensely. "But this is a decision he'll have to make himself—whether he wants to be a talented quitter or a humble man of strength." And then Al listened as his father prayed.

"Lord, you've given Al so much talent. But, Lord, his character is just not what it should be. Please, help him, please, to become like You— the great God of creation—who humbled Yourself to the point of living with weak, arrogant sinners who rejected You. . ."

Al could not listen anymore. His eyes were filled with water, and his stomach was churning with deep emotion begging for release. He ran into his room, closed the door, then threw himself on his bed, giving full expression to the violent sobs within.

The next morning at breakfast, Al quietly took his place at the table. After staring intently at his orange juice for over a minute, he broke the silence, still staring at the glass.

"I've been a real fool. But I think I've learned something." He wanted to say more but could not. Emotions deeper than any he had ever felt, strange, confusing, but somehow clean-feeling emotions, overwhelmed him. As he rose from the table and reached for his schoolbooks, which were sitting on the kitchen counter, he felt his dad's strong hand warmly embrace his shoulder. He turned and looked into moist, deeply understanding, and lovingly proud eyes. In that instant, his already full and deep emotions nearly burst from his body in a shout of incredible joy. Then a sense of awkward embarrassment took over, and he settled for grabbing his father's arm tightly for a second, then kissed his mother, and without a word, left for school.

When the final class bell rang, Al strode purposefully to the football team's locker room. The few players who were already suiting up eyed him, then turned away. Al never broke step as he aimed straight for the coach's office.

"Come in," Coach Taylor called out in response to Al's knock.

Al opened the frosted glass door and walked up to the coach's desk. Taylor neither smiled nor frowned. "Sit down, Al," he said.

"Coach, I came here to apologize. I was wrong to quit trying. Every guy on our team is a better man than me because they kept trying. I want to apologize to them for letting them down and," Al hesitated, "if you'll have me, I'd like to play for the Hustlers again."

Coach Taylor never changed his expression as he stood up, walked, to the door, turned, and said, "Al, come with me." Al obediently followed.

By this time, most of the players had arrived for practice and were changing into scrimmage uniforms. The coach barked, "All you guys, everyone, over here. We're having a meeting."

The players walked over, looking uncertainly at

Al. When they were all in the vicinity of the coach's office, some standing, others sitting on the benches. Coach Taylor nodded to Al and said, "You're on."

Al gulped, fumbled over a few beginning noises, then with a clear voice said, "Guys, I really blew it. I let you down. I don't deserve to play on this team, but I want to. If you'll let me come back, I'll do my best."

Before the players had a chance to respond, Taylor spoke. "Al, what you've done is inexcusable. I will not permit you to resume play without penalty. If the players agree to your coming back on the team, I'll let you practice with us for two weeks but you won't play in the next two games. If you prove that you're really with us, you can suit up for the third game."

Turning to the players, Coach Taylor asked, "Gentlemen, it's up to you. If you are willing to have Al return under the terms I just stated, raise your hand."

Al was trembling as he looked over the room full of boys. Slowly, one by one, hands were lifted into the air until every player voted that Al could return—every player, that is, except one. Clark Dentworth's arm remained stiffly at his side.

"OK, Al, the vote is yes. Get dressed."

For the next two weeks, Al pushed to his limit

in the practice sessions. Never had he strained so hard to produce. He spent much of his time working with a reluctant Clark Dentworth, showing him how to fall back quickly into the pocket, set, then pass. Clark soon warmed up to his teacher and, in spite of unyielding clumsiness, began to learn something about quarterbacking.

The next two games proved to be the Hustlers' best efforts in their history. They were defeated in the first by only one touchdown and a field goal and in the second by only a field goal. Dentworth's statistics would never tempt a college coach, but for him they were impressive—two fumbles, three interceptions, six completed passes, and twenty-four yards gained on the ground. After a four-yard touchdown pass in the second game, he ran over to the coach and bubbled, "Change my vote on Scabbard to yes."

The third weekend finally arrived. The seemingly endless suspension was lifted. It was Saturday afternoon. Blue skies laced with a few billowy clouds looked down on a buzzing, restless, excited mass of Hustler fans filling the bleachers. Word had spread into every corner of Hamilton's hallways: Al Scabbard was back. One quiet, serious-looking man sat motionless on the top bleacher, leaning forward with both elbows resting on his knees. Only a slight tapping of his left foot disturbed his almost rigid position.

The Hustlers won the toss. Derek Adams scampered backward to receive the opening kick. The wildly turning pigskin eluded his frantic grasp and bounced toward the Hustlers' goal. Adams fell on it at his own 16-yard line. Three blue-shirted Mavericks from Marple Junior High smothered Adams immediately. Their team, tied for second in the Northeast Regional Conference, was fast.

On the first play from center, Scabbard threw a bomb, a perfect forty-yard spiral lofted beautifully into the outstretched arms of Gary Brent. He dropped it.

Mr. Scabbard's foot picked up the pace.

When Gary returned to the huddle, Al gave him a friendly slap on the shoulder and said, "I underthrew it. This time we'll get it right. Same play. Let's go."

Scabbard drifted back into the pocket. Another perfect pass. Brent's eager arms wrapped around the ball, and he dashed all the way down to the Maverick's 4-yard line.

In the next three plays from scrimmage, Al handed off twice to his backfield for a net loss of eight yards and bulleted a pass off the chest of his tight end. Fourth down and twelve yards to go for a score.

The snap from center. Al danced back, caught a glimpse of Brent through three blue shirts, then spotted an opening to the left, and shot through the hole toward the goal. One linebacker appeared to block his path. Al's legs were churning like pistons. When Al and the linebacker collided, a 185-pound body wrapped in a blue shirt dropped with a thud on the turf. Scabbard crossed the goal. Score: Hamilton 6, Mavericks 0.

Hamilton's Hustlers played ball that day like never before. Gary Brent dropped only four of thirteen well-thrown passes. Derek Adams fumbled once more but held onto three long punts and ran them back for six, twenty-four, and fifteen yards respectively.

Al looked more like a seasoned college quarterback playing for a front-running team than like a young teenager competing with a last place junior high squad. The bleachers roared with astonished excitement when Al hurled a thirty-five-yard pass to Gary Brent, and broke into a mad frenzy when Al twisted his way through a handful of blue-shirted defenders for a touchdown run of eighty yards.

Although much improved, Al's teammates were something less then sensational. But each time one of the Hustlers' muffed a play, Al smiled confidently and encouraged the team to keep on hustling.

The Hustlers' defense performed valiantly, but the Maverick offensive backfield was good. With twenty seconds to go in the game, the Hustlers trailed by four points, 28-24. Al called his team to a huddle behind their own 18-yard line. He knelt on one knee and looked up into ten eager, expectant faces.

"Gary, go all the way. Turn on the speed and I'll hit you downfield. Let's go."

The center's hands trembled over the ball. He snapped it underneath Al's waiting hands and onto the ground. Al seized it quickly and floated back. He fled to the right, giving Gary time to get further downfield. Gary was turning it on. He had gained two steps on his defender. Al cocked his arm and let fly. He uncorked a forty-five-yard pass that spiraled perfectly into Gary's extended arms. Gary held onto that ball like a mother carrying a child through a fire, and dashed out of reach of two desperate Mavericks, hot in pursuit. With two seconds to go in the game, Gary's legs crossed over the end stripe for the final score of the game. The scoreboard told the story—Hustlers 30, Opponents 28.

No one really noticed that on the try for point after touchdown, the snap from center soared high over the kneeling receiver's arms. Tony Fortosi, the Hustlers' kicker, fell on the ball. The game was over.

When the gun sounded, pandemonium filled the grandstands. Hundreds of eager fans raced